**Lose yourself in a heartrending duet
from Lucy Clark…**

SAVING TWIN BABIES

WEDDING ON THE BABY WARD

Delivering these premature conjoined twins
is neonatal specialist Miles Trevellion's
only priority—the compellingly
beautiful Dr Janessa Austen can be
nothing more than his colleague. For now…

SPECIAL CARE BABY MIRACLE

New mum Sheena's tiny girls
are fighting for their lives, and
paediatric surgeon Will Beckman is the man
to save them! Sheena's hoping for two little
miracles—but perhaps an unexpected
third dream might also come true…

SAVING TWIN BABIES

*Only the world's most renowned doctors—
and a miracle or two—
can save these tiny twins.*

**Both titles are available this month
from Mills & Boon Medical™ Romance.**

Dear Reader

Babies are always so cute but beautiful twin girls who are born conjoined can really capture your heart. Ellie and Sarah are two little girls who came into the world and unbeknownst to them, ended up uniting four very special people.

Janessa and Miles were so much fun to write, especially the part about making Janessa a pilot. After being given a joy-ride flight in a tiger moth biplane as a birthday present, we knew the experience was one that needed to be relayed in a book. The airfield where Janessa flies her plane is one of our favourite places to visit and part of the book was even typed there, sipping a nice cup of coffee on a pleasant Spring day while the lovely old planes take to the skies.

Sheena and Will brought their own set of unique challenges to the story. For Sheena, going through not only the pregnancy but the long awaited separation of her gorgeous twin girls was gut wrenching to write, especially after reading and researching how parents feel when faced with such situations. With Will by her side, loving and caring for not only her but the girls as well, Sheena was able to get the happily ever after she so richly deserved.

We hope you enjoy reading about these special babies who have brought together two couples who were made for each other.

Warmest regards,

Lucy

WEDDING ON THE BABY WARD

BY
LUCY CLARK

First published in Great Britain 2011
by Mills & Boon, an imprint of Harlequin (UK) Limited.
Large Print edition 2012
Harlequin (UK) Limited, Eton House,
18-24 Paradise Road, Richmond, Surrey TW9 1SR

© Anne and Peter Clark 2011

ISBN: 978 0 263 22430 6

Harlequin (UK) policy is to use papers that are natural, renewable and recyclable products and made from wood grown in sustainable forests. The logging and manufacturing process conform to the legal environmental regulations of the country of origin.

Printed and bound in Great Britain
by CPI Antony Rowe, Chippenham, Wiltshire

Lucy Clark is actually a husband-and-wife writing team. They enjoy taking holidays with their children, during which they discuss and develop new ideas for their books using the fantastic Australian scenery. They use their daily walks to talk over characterisation and fine details of the wonderful stories they produce, and are avid movie buffs. They live on the edge of a popular wine district in South Australia with their two children, and enjoy spending family time together at weekends.

Recent titles by the same author:

DOCTOR DIAMOND IN THE ROUGH
THE DOCTOR'S SOCIETY SWEETHEART
THE DOCTOR'S DOUBLE TROUBLE

**These titles are also available in ebook format
from www.millsandboon.co.uk**

For Lili and Mat—
who share the same warped and
silly sense of humour as us.
Thanks for making us feel normal!
—*Hosea* 14:9

CHAPTER ONE

'JANESSA. Phone,' an agency nurse called. 'It's the maternity ward. They say it's urgent.'

'I'm a little busy,' Janessa Austen replied, not taking her attention from her latest patient. The Adelaide Mercy NICU had quite a few of the regular nurses off sick today and while the nursing agency had provided staff to keep things running, these nurses weren't trained in NICU procedure. 'Find out what the situation is and I'll get someone to go to Maternity as soon as possible.'

Both Janessa and Kaycee, one of her top NICU nurses, stood next to the open cot of the tiny twenty-six-week-old baby girl who was in need of urgent medical attention. Baby Taneesha had been born only twenty minutes ago and had been intubated and rushed from the delivery suite down the corridor to the NICU where the brave little soul continued to fight for her life. The staff were giving her breaths via the Neopuff to keep her alive while they organised the ventilator.

'Kaycee, we need some surfactant,' Janessa ordered. 'It works so well on these tiny stiff lungs,' she mused as she continued to work. Whilst it had been 'one of those days', Janessa wasn't about to lose a patient, not to fatigue nor interrupting phone calls.

'Come on, Taneesha,' Janessa said with loving determination. 'Hang in there, sweetie. You can do it.' While she crooned to the baby, Janessa's hands were working rapidly. 'What are the oxygen saturations?' she asked, her gaze focused on what she was doing.

'Eighty per cent,' Kaycee replied as she began to increase the oxygen levels.

'How's that surfactant coming along? We need to get that moisture into the lungs, stat.'

Kaycee was working quickly and handed the syringe to Janessa who administered the liquid into the endo-trachael tube. A few minutes later the oxygen saturations went up as Taneesha's breathing started to improve. Kaycee did the observations once more as the agency nurse came over to Janessa.

'Maternity don't need you to send anyone up,' the nurse reported. It was around lunchtime, her first day on the job, and she'd been thrown in at the deep end. Still, Janessa couldn't help that. They'd already had three babies born within the last hour, all of whom had come directly to the NICU, the ward clerk was out on her lunch break and the rest of the staff were either assisting in the delivery suites or monitoring other little babies. Today, the NICU's forty-four-cot ward was most definitely full to capacity.

'What's the problem, then?' Janessa asked, still focused on Taneesha.

'There was an emergency.' The nurse consulted a piece of paper in her hand. 'A baby by the name of Joey. Apparently, his lips started to turn blue.'

'Not again.' Janessa sighed and shook her head. 'Has he been attended to?'

'Um... They said the doctor is bringing him down.'

'The doctor? Doctor who?' Janessa asked.

'Excuse me! Assistance required. Over here,' a deep male voice said from the entrance to the NICU, and Janessa glanced over briefly to see a man in a rumpled suit walking into the unit, pushing a baby's crib. She didn't know who he was but she knew who the baby was.

'That'll be Joey.' Janessa looked at the agency nurse. 'Go and bring him in. Put him...' she quickly scanned the NICU '...bay two for now.' She returned her attention to Taneesha, while checking the blood gas results. The agency nurse hovered uncertainly for a moment before heading over to where the man was already pushing Joey's crib into the NICU, not waiting for anyone.

'Come this way. B-Bay two,' the agency nurse stammered.

'Right. Bay two. Well…lead on,' the man said with a hint of impatience as he removed his jacket and tossed it carelessly onto a desk. Thankfully, his tone wasn't loud but it was definitely insistent and Janessa hoped the sensitive babies in the NICU didn't pick up on the disruption. The last thing any of them wanted right now was a chain reaction of one baby after the other crying in the need for attention and comfort.

'Had to happen on a day when we're short-staffed,' Janessa mumbled.

'Oxygen, stat,' the male doctor ordered. 'Baby is cyanotic. No, no, no. Thirty per cent oxygen,' he growled at the nurse. 'Don't you even know that much?' He shook his head and took over.

'Obs?' Janessa asked, concentrating on blocking out the larger-than-life man who was creating havoc in her NICU. She wasn't the type of woman to allow her temper to get the better of her—in fact, she prided herself on having good control over all her faculties—but today, with the lack of sleep and her very early morning start, the edges were starting to fray.

Kaycee started the obs as Janessa rechecked the fluids that would help Taneesha. She wanted to look up, to check out what was happening in *her* unit, but she remained steadfastly by Taneesha's side. 'That's it, Taneesha. Good girl. You keep fighting.' Janessa looked at Kaycee.

'Her oxygen saturations are now stable,' Kaycee reported after quickly doing the observations, and Janessa let out a sigh of thanks. 'I'll go see what the commotion is all about.'

'No. It's OK.' Janessa quickly pulled off her gloves and rubbed her bare hand over Taneesha's tiny body, pleased to note that the skin was not only a much better colour but much, much warmer than before. 'There you go, love,' she whispered to the babe, before glancing at Kaycee. 'Stay and monitor Taneesha for me.' Janessa reached for another pair of gloves. 'I'll go see what's happening with Joey.' She jerked her head towards the commotion. 'And can we perhaps see if Ray's finished assisting in the delivery suite? It would be great to have him back here in the unit.'

'I'll see to it,' Kaycee responded, and as Janessa headed towards the newest arrival in the NICU, she took one calming breath, knowing she could leave the running of things in Kaycee's more than capable hands while she pulled strength from thin air to concentrate on the latest event in her already overly hectic day. She'd been on the go since about four o'clock that morning and as it was now just after one o'clock in the afternoon, her exhaustion level was steadily on the rise.

'No. That's the wrong-size cannula. This is ridiculous,' the man was saying to the agency nurse, who looked completely flustered and about ready to burst into tears. 'Go away. I'll do it myself.'

'What's the status?' Janessa asked smoothly, after giving a dismissive nod to the agency nurse. The unit was stressful enough at the moment and the sooner she could defuse the situation, the better.

'The status is to find someone in this place to assist me, preferably before this baby dies.'

Janessa unhooked her stethoscope from around her neck and put the eartips into her ears, before listening closely to Joey's chest. She heard the rasping instantly and sighed at her little charge. Without another word she went to a nearby cupboard, pulling out the correct equipment they would need.

'He needs a chest X-ray. We need to see if this baby has aspirated.'

'What happened?'

'I was in Maternity, reviewing a patient, when I

noticed this chap coughing. I went to check and noticed he was cyanotic. Naturally, I thought he needed treatment so had him brought down here, but apparently...' he glanced pointedly at Janessa '...this NICU is understaffed and no doubt requires a full review.'

Janessa tried her hardest not to bristle at the way he was speaking to her, the way he was looking at her and the way he was treating her. It was clear by the way he was handling the medical equipment that he was a doctor. In another brief glance, she took in his seriously creased navy trousers and crinkled white shirt covering his firm torso, a college tie, which was knotted loosely, and beneath that his top shirt button was undone. His whole attire screamed 'surgeon' and a dishevelled one at that. What on earth had he been doing before arriving here in her unit?

Dr Whoever-he-was had just finished rolling up the sleeves of his shirt, right past his elbows and was washing his hands. As he reached for a pair of gloves, Janessa gave him a quick once-over and although he appeared incredibly handsome, with short dark brown hair and a square jaw complete with a cleft in his chin, his attitude was too arrogant for her taste.

'All hospitals are understaffed,' Janessa remarked

quietly and matter-of-factly as she looped the stethoscope around her neck. She wouldn't allow herself to be embroiled in a slanging match with this man. She was a professional and she had a job to do. 'Right, Joey, let's get you sorted.'

'Joey? My name is Dr Trevellion, not Joey,' he growled, his words clipped yet measured, indicating he knew not to raise his tone in case he upset the babies.

Momentarily stunned, Janessa met his gaze, her eyebrows raised as her insides did a little nervous flip at this news. Dr Trevellion! She'd known he was coming to Adelaide Mercy hospital for six months as she'd been the one to initially request his presence, and while she'd read his articles and followed his career, she never would have connected the photograph of the clean, crisp professional portrayed in medical journals to the crumpled, crabby man in her NICU.

Here he was. Australian specialist. The great and marvellous—and obviously arrogant and impatient—Dr Miles Trevellion. In *her* NICU! Great. It was just what she didn't need added to her impossibly draining day. Then again, she supposed as he was one of the world's leading NICU specialists, she should have expected the arrogance and self-importance he seemed to exude, but it didn't, however, change the fact that little Joey required their expertise.

'Joey is the baby's name, Dr Trevellion,' she pointed out, both of them busy as they prepared to treat Joey. 'He was here in the unit two weeks ago, doing this same old party trick, but apparently he's back for a repeat performance.'

'He's done it before?' Dr Trevellion clenched his square jaw in disapproval. 'Then why wasn't he here in the unit, receiving the proper treatment, instead of in the ward, in the hands of an inexperienced mother?' The exasperation in his tone was evident.

Janessa's muscles instantly tensed at his words and she ground her teeth. 'You may regard Joey's mother as inexperienced but I'll have you know that Adelaide Mercy prides itself on providing the best instruction and support for every mother who comes through our doors.'

'So you pushed him up to the maternity ward because there wasn't room for him here?'

'On the contrary. Joey's mother needs to learn how to deal with this situation. The fact that Joey's been having breathing difficulties is the main reason why they haven't been discharged yet. We couldn't rule out something like this happening again and I'll have you know that Joey was clinically stable before being released to the maternity ward.'

'Well, he's not now. Let's get an IV line in and monitor him properly.'

Janessa glanced at Dr Trevellion, noting that his tone had mellowed slightly and now, instead of looking annoyed and impatient, he simply looked tired and exhausted, and she wondered exactly when he'd arrived, not only at Adelaide Mercy hospital but, more importantly, when he'd arrived in Australia. She certainly hoped he hadn't come here directly from an international flight but now that she took in his attire, she guessed her assumptions were fairly accurate. He would have wanted to make his own assessment on the yet-to-be delivered conjoined twins he'd been appointed to care for. If their positions had been reversed, Janessa would have gone directly to the hospital from the airport as well.

The only words spoken between the two of them were instructions and Janessa found Dr Miles Trevellion to be clear and direct. That was good given that she'd be working with him for the next six months. A thrill of excitement swept through her at the realisation that she was standing opposite the great neonate surgeon yet she was grounded enough not to let it go to her head.

'There you go, little guy,' Dr Trevellion said softly about five minutes later when Joey started to stabilise, the rasping in his chest now beginning to settle into a more normal rhythm. Dr Trevellion took off his gloves and gently touched the baby's skin, showing such intense caring that Janessa was momentarily stunned.

He cared. He had a heart and it could be touched. Watching him, the way he interacted with little Joey, was enough to restore her faith in him. She'd never doubted his abilities but seeing him speaking so softly to the babe, watching the tender way he touched the little boy's body, showed her that he was a man who really did care about his patients.

'Hey, Nessa. Kaycee said you needed my help,' a man in his late forties, with slightly greying hair and the occasional hint of a lilting Scottish accent, said as he sauntered towards them. Janessa looked away from Miles Trevellion, only belatedly realising she'd been staring at him.

'Oh, hi, Ray. No. We're fine here. Situation stabilised. But allow me to introduce you to Dr Trevellion.'

Ray's bushy eyebrows shot up at the news. 'Trevellion? Really? *The* same Dr Trevellion who's come here to look after our Sheena's conjoined twins?' Without waiting for an answer, he continued, 'In that case, welcome to Adelaide Mercy and to the NICU.' Ray heartily shook the other man's hand. 'We're so glad to have you on our team, aren't we, Nessa?'

'Very.' Janessa pulled off her gloves and stepped back from the crib. 'Ray, would you mind calling up to the ward to let them know we'll be keeping Joey for at least the next twenty-four hours,' she requested.

'Right you are, lassie. Say, why don't the two of you go and have a cuppa, eh? I'm sure Dr Trevellion would relish the chance to talk about our Sheena, given that's the reason why he's come here in the first place.'

'You took the words right out of my mouth,' she agreed. 'We'd best do it while the unit is a relatively quiet and settled. Goodness knows, that can change at any given moment.' Janessa looked to the handsome newcomer and spread her hand wide, indicating the way to her office. 'Shall we?'

'What? You?' He looked from Ray to Janessa. 'You're joking, right? You're just a nurse.'

'*Just* a nurse?' She frowned at him. 'That's a phrase you'd better not bandy around too much, Dr Trevellion. I'll have you know that our full-time senior nurses are the best in Australia. There's Ray here, who is always so calm, cool and collected.' She pointed. 'Over there we have Kaycee, who is forever brilliant and a walking encyclopaedia, and the woman who's just walked into the ward, heading for the sink, is Helena.'

'She's going to retire at the end of the year,' Ray added. 'Not sure what we're going to do without her. She's such a mother-hen, always looking after her chicks, and I'm not just talking about the young mums who are constantly in the unit with their ill wee ones—she's a mother to the staff as well.'

'My senior three.' Janessa nodded.

Dr Trevellion was still looking at her but this time there was amused disbelief in his eyes. '*You're* really the head of the NICU? But you look about nineteen years old!'

Ray chuckled. 'That she does, but don't let the outward demeanour fool you. Our Janessa is well trained, highly intelligent and always in control.'

'Thank you, Ray,' Janessa remarked, feeling extremely self-conscious.

'*You're* Janessa Austen?' Miles couldn't disguise his utter astonishment. His expression should have amused her, and probably on another day it might have, but now that the emergencies seemed to have settled down, fatigue and hunger were starting to gnaw at her again.

'I've heard all about you,' he continued as he followed her. 'Although for some unfathomable reason, I expected you to be…' He stopped, trying his best to be diplomatic but realising he'd already failed. His mind was still fuzzy from the travelling he'd done during the past thirty hours. 'Older,' he finished.

'I may look young, Dr Trevellion, but I can safely assure you,' she said as they walked into her office, 'that I am fully qualified to *be* the head of the NICU.' She closed the door behind her and motioned to the seat opposite her desk. Dr Trevellion stared at her and it seemed to take a few seconds for her words to sink in and for him to realise that she was indeed quite serious.

She *was* Janessa Austen and this *was* her NICU. 'Then it must be said, Dr Austen, that you carry your age exceedingly well.' His tone was rich, deep and smooth as he delivered the compliment. A complete contrast from the way he'd spoken when he'd first entered the unit, and for a second the change almost put Janessa off balance.

'Thank you.' She'd be unwise to put any credence in the compliment, even though she wanted to be-cause, quite simply, no man had complimented her in such a very long time. However, this man was her new colleague, at least for the next six months that he would remain at Adelaide Mercy hospital.

He'd come specifically to guide the neonate team through the delivery and subsequent surgeries of the conjoined twins who were due to be born within the next few weeks. He would also be doing some research, some lecturing and helping out in the NICU when his schedule permitted. Allowing herself to become distracted by his compliments, by his good looks and by his status was out of the question. Brisk, clear and professional. That was the only type of relationship she wanted with him.

'Please, won't you sit down?' She again proffered the chair. 'You must be tired.'

'Do I look tired?' he asked as he relented and sat in the chair opposite her, a hint of his earlier impatience returning. His back was straight, his shoulders broad and they really filled out the clothes he wore. Janessa swallowed and looked away from his body to his annoyed blue eyes.

'Yes, as a matter of fact, you do,' she replied honestly. 'My guess is that you've probably come from the airport straight to the hospital in order to check on the conjoined twins.'

'That is what I've been hired to do.'

'Of course.' She clasped her hands tightly together and placed them carefully onto her desk as she controlled her breathing. It wasn't what he was saying that was starting to grate on her nerves but *how* he was saying it. His tone was clipped and mildly annoyed and she didn't appreciate it at all but she could also hear the fatigue hidden beneath and that was reason enough for her to cut him some slack...that and the fact that she would be working closely with him. It would be ridiculous to get off on the wrong foot. 'Would you prefer a cup of coffee instead of tea?' she offered.

'I don't want a drink. I didn't come here for polite pleasantries.'

'Obviously,' she remarked under her breath.

'Pardon?'

She pasted on a polite smile. 'Nothing. So, I take it you've already seen Sheena?'

'Yes,' he grumbled with increasing impatience. 'That's why I was in Maternity and was able to bring that sick little baby to the NICU before things got worse.' Irritated, unable to sit, Dr Trevellion stood, his presence almost filling her small office as he paced back and forth.

She recalled the way she'd pored over the plethora of articles he'd written over the years, how he'd reported on his vast experience working with many different teams in the caring practices and surgical breakthroughs with conjoined twins. He was a highly reputed specialist, a man of incredible knowledge, and she had to admit to being a little disappointed in finding him so blusterous. She sincerely hoped it was merely the jet lag talking and that their entire working relationship wasn't going to be this antagonistic.

Thinking of her amazing friend Sheena, who was the mother-to-be of the conjoined twins, Janessa forced herself to take a calming breath before remarking, 'I do thank you for bringing Joey to the NICU. Your prompt action and attention were invaluable to his health and now we can continue to monitor his progress more closely.'

Dr Trevellion stopped pacing and turned to glare at her, his blue eyes even more piercing than before. 'Don't you dare hand me that polite diplomatic claptrap. I don't appreciate it one bit. The fact of the matter is that if this NICU is to be the primary provider for conjoined twins, your unit needs to be run with a tighter grip on the expectations placed upon it not only by the hospital at large but by the needs of the patients.'

Janessa's eyes opened wider at his words. How dared he? And she'd been trying to be nice. 'And *I* don't appreciate,' she interjected when he paused to drag in a breath to continue his blustering, 'visiting consultants who barge into *my* unit, demanding instant attention and upsetting my staff. My unit runs effectively and efficiently and I'll thank you kindly not to come in here with your unfounded accusations and over-inflated ego.' While she spoke, she kept her voice clear but firm. Yelling and bawling people out was definitely not Janessa's style but neither was she a doormat. She hadn't achieved her position as head of unit simply by her good looks. She could be direct and as stubborn as the next man when it was called for.

Slowly she rose to her full height of five feet eight inches and placed her hands on her desk as she met his gaze with determination and veiled anger. 'You may have more experience than any of us when it comes to conjoined twins, Dr Trevellion, but that is no reason for you to believe that you're also employed to harness more productivity from the Adelaide Mercy NICU. You are not. You are here for the next six months as a visiting consultant, not head of unit, not even as a permanent member of staff and I'll thank you kindly to keep your comments to those of a professional nature without adding an insulting slur to everything you say.'

He raised one eyebrow at her and for an instant she thought she saw his lips twitch into a bit of a smile. The action confused her. Was he cross with her or was there something else happening here? She had the strangest feeling that he was testing the waters, trying to gauge her personality. If that was the case, she still didn't like it. 'In other words, if I can't say anything nice, don't say anything at all?'

She lifted her chin a little higher, defiance flashing in her eyes. It was then and only then that Miles actually started to realise that whilst his new colleague might indeed look very young, she most certainly wasn't. There was wisdom in her eyes that said he'd almost pushed her to the brink of keeping her temper in check. She was doing very well at controlling it, and he had to admit he admired her style.

'If you like.' Her tone was still controlled, still firm and still on fire—a fire that was directed solely at him.

'Well, then.' He inclined his head towards her. 'I'll bid you *adieu*.' He turned and had taken but three steps towards her door, his back ramrod straight, his broad shoulders square, the material of his white shirt pulled tightly around his firm torso, when Janessa spoke again, her voice brisk, efficient and polite.

'Thank you for your assistance, Dr Trevellion. I'll see you at the prep meeting tomorrow morning.'

Dr Trevellion didn't speak a word but merely continued on his way.

As she watched him go, Janessa didn't move. Instead she counted slowly to ten inside her head, hoping to calm her nerves. It didn't work. She counted to twenty and started to feel a little better. Exhaling and sinking back into her chair, she picked up a piece of scrap paper from the recycle bin and ripped it into tiny shreds, the action doing a lot to calm her frazzled nerves.

Miles Trevellion was one of the finest leading NICU specialists in the field. He was a qualified vascular surgeon who would be caring for Sheena Woodcombe's conjoined twins, which were scheduled for delivery by Caesarean section in two weeks' time. Janessa was the second NICU specialist in charge—a placement she was determined to keep given that Sheena was like a sister to her.

She sat there for a whole two minutes, her door open, making her feel highly exposed even though no one walked by. She simply couldn't believe how insufferable Miles Trevellion had turned out to be. She had been initially excited to learn of his appointment and then nervous at the prospect of working alongside the great man. Now, she wasn't even looking forward to their first preparation meeting tomorrow morning.

'It doesn't matter what you want,' she told herself sternly as she rose from the desk. Sheena was the one who mattered and she wasn't going to let her friend down. The two women had met on their first day of medical school and although Janessa had pursued neonatology and Sheena paediatrics, their friendship had remained solid.

They knew each other's history. Together they'd

celebrated the good times and cried through the bad. Sheena had been the person who had helped rebuild Janessa's confidence all those years ago, who had supported her when her father had died and who had been the first person on the scene when Janessa's house had burnt to the ground eight months ago.

In return, Janessa had been there for Sheena, through thick and thin. Bridesmaid at her wedding, confidante throughout Sheena's rocky marriage and supporter through the present divorce proceedings. Sheena's life was now upside down, and Janessa was determined to be by her side.

Being an integral part of the neonatal team responsible for the care of the conjoined twins once they were born was not only going to be one of the highlights of her career but also an esteemed privilege for in the future she would be a strong presence of the twins' lives.

She hadn't been able to save her own child, the baby born far too early. At only nineteen years old, she'd given birth to a tiny premature baby who hadn't been strong enough to survive. She'd been a young, inexperienced teenage mother whose darling little boy, Connor, hadn't been strong enough to fight for his life. Her young marriage hadn't survived the death of the baby but her determination to specialise in the field of neonatology had started to evolve.

The staff who had looked after her when Connor had been born, the specialists who had cared for him, fighting for his life, doing everything they could, had been her inspiration to do well in her classes. She had wanted to be like them, to be able to make a difference in someone else's life, to help and support young mothers and to fight for the lives of the little tiny babies who were born weeks before their due dates.

With supportive parents, she'd started medical school, only to have her mother pass away within that first year. Ultimately, it was her friendship with Sheena that had helped her through those difficult years.

Now she would do everything she could for her friend and those beautiful babies. She would be a part of their lives, their Aunty Nessa, who would love them and spoil them, and that was an honour she didn't take at all lightly.

She was now a specialist, able to help young mothers such as she had been. She had the knowledge, she had the experience and she would provide the best care for those babies, alongside her new colleague. Miles Trevellion would no doubt be the thorn in her side throughout this experience, given the man appeared to have an ego the size of Australia. He was good looking—of that there was no doubt.

He was highly skilled and intelligent—that was not in question. But in instilling confidence and gaining respect of his colleagues? On that front, it appeared he was seriously lacking.

Miles Trevellion was the specialist, the surgeon, the man who was going to ensure those two little girls were able to live normal lives, and to that end Janessa would have to bite her tongue if he offended or upset her. The babies and Sheena were the important ones in this scenario and there was no way she was going to let any of them down.

CHAPTER TWO

MUCH later that day, once life in the unit had settled to a more normal level, Janessa made her way to the maternity ward to check on Sheena.

'Did you meet him?' Sheena asked eagerly as soon as Janessa came into the private room. As Sheena was a practising paediatrician at Adelaide Mercy, now on maternity leave, it was only right that she have top-of-the-line care.

'Who?' She was fairly certain Sheena was referring to Miles Trevellion, the man whom she'd been hard pressed to stop thinking about ever since he'd made such a dramatic entrance into her life.

'Who? Are you blind, deaf and dumb?'

Janessa sat in the chair beside the bed and closed her eyes. 'I feel it. Who are we talking about?'

'Miles Trevellion, of course. Isn't he charming?'

Janessa frowned but kept her eyes closed, an image of the man they were talking about swimming easily to mind. 'Not exactly the word I'd use to describe him.'

'It is for me. And he's sexy and good-looking—and those eyes...' Sheena sighed with longing, and when Janessa opened her eyes to look at her friend she saw that the woman's hands were clasped romantically together and held close towards her heart...or as close as she could get due to her enlarged abdomen.

'He can check on me any time he feels like it,' she drawled, the words punctuated with little sighs.

Janessa shook her head then chuckled at her friend. 'You should already know what he looked like. Didn't you work with him years ago when you did your overseas placement in Philadelphia?'

'I did and that's where I also met Will.'

'Ahh...the real love of your life. No wonder you didn't talk about Miles that much when you arrived back in Australia. You were too busy pining over Will.'

'Yep. Will. The man who didn't want me,' Sheena continued, before flicking her fingers as though to rid herself of the memory. 'But Miles...now, he was always quite the catch, even back then. So gorgeous and suave, and let me tell you, Nessa, he's improved with age.' Sheena waggled her eyebrows up and down.

'Well, I'm glad you like him. It's important that you like him. After all, as far as conjoined twins go, he's the expert.' And, therefore, she told herself, probably entitled to be arrogant and insufferable. For the job he needed to do, he no doubt needed a big ego as well. Still, she couldn't help reflecting on the small smile she'd seen touch his lips and wondered what it might be like to see him really smile. She shook her head, as though to clear it.

'You don't like him?' Sheena was stunned.

'It doesn't matter whether I like him or not, Sheenie. I respect him for his intelligence and I'm happy to learn he clearly has a decent bedside manner, given the way you're gushing about him.'

'Oh, he's charming all right. It's been ten years since I last saw him. We worked together for just under a month and even back then he had the habit of setting every woman's heart fluttering with his striking good looks and deep voice and sexy walk and—'

Janessa held up her hands. 'All right, all right. I get the point.' Because she really did. She could quite see, in the looks department, that Miles Trevellion had a lot going for him, but for her money she was attracted to men who had manners, charm and intellect. Well, she had to admit that Miles also had intellect, of that there was no doubt, but manners and charm? She'd yet to see what Sheena was talking about.

'So why don't you like him?' Sheena asked.

Janessa paused for a moment, choosing her words carefully. 'It's not that I don't like him per se, I hardly know the man.'

'But you were looking forward to him coming? To meeting him. You were the one who suggested we ask him to come to Adelaide Mercy in the first place, remember? And then you brought in a swag of his articles for me to read.' Sheena pointed to the pile of medical journals in the opened top drawer by the bed. Janessa instantly leaned over and closed the drawer, not wanting to dwell on the way she'd gushed about the man and his genius.

She could see she needed to define her present feelings towards Miles Trevellion in order to get Sheena off her back. 'OK. I have no problem admitting I admire him as a professional. If I find him a little overbearing and slightly dictatorial, that's my personal problem. Our job—the job Dr Trevellion and I need to focus on—is looking after your girls, and that's something we'll be doing to the highest standards.'

'You're still being cagey and I know that means I'm not going to get much else out of you, so instead tell me all about the medical emergency that happened here around lunchtime. Is everything all right?'

'Yes. All under control. Baby is fine. Dr Trevellion saved the day.'

'Great.' Sheena didn't sound at all happy. 'And I missed it, of course, because I'm stuck here, not allowed to get out of bed and needing to have my catheter bag changed almost hourly because my bladder is the size of a peanut, which means I only heard the news second hand,' Sheena grumbled. 'The nurses, who usually gossip about everything, have told me hardly anything. It's entirely not fair that as a practising paediatrician and one who is a valued member of staff at this very hospital, I'm not all that impressed about whoever has given the "gag" order surrounding me.'

'That would be me and you're a paediatrician who is on *maternity leave*.' Janessa stood and instantly picked up her friend's wrist, checking her pulse. 'You're not allowed to be worried or stressed or concerned or anything else about the goings-on in the hospital, Sheenie, and you know that. We've discussed it.'

'My blood pressure is fine,' Sheena grumped.

'Actually, it's a little raised.'

'That's because you won't tell me what's going on. I'm just a human incubator. Nothing more. Nothing less.'

Janessa smiled. 'Don't say that. You know you

don't mean it. You mean everything to these babies and they mean everything to you. Your girls need you, Sheena, you're their world. You're the only one who can really protect them and you do that by lying here and doing nothing. We can only do so much to help the girls and therefore need to keep you as calm and controlled as possible. The gag order is in place because I can't have you getting stressed about things you would ordinarily have some control over. You're an amazing paediatrician, Sheenie, but you're on maternity leave and I need you to *leave* hospital matters alone.'

'But sometimes telling me what's happening actually decreases the risk of my blood pressure going up because I'm not frustrated from being kept in the dark,' Sheena quickly pointed out.

Janessa paused for a moment before shaking her head. 'It's all under control. Nothing to report. Now, before I forget, the special baby clothes that we picked out from the catalogue should be here within the next few days. I received an email telling me they were being shipped so we can look forward to their arrival soon.'

'I can hardly remember what we ordered.' Sheena frowned, still not happy that Janessa had cut off her sources of information.

'Well, let me remind you. There was a pretty pink

dress with frills and...' As the two of them sat there, talking about baby clothes, Janessa started to feel the stress of her day begin to ease. It had been a long, long day, made even longer with the arrival of Miles Trevellion, who she hadn't expected to see until tomorrow at their prep meeting.

'Now,' she said, standing to hug her friend, 'you'll be due for growth hormone injections soon because we need these little girls as fit and as healthy as possible, so settle down and get some sleep.'

'Ha. My girls may be literally joined at the hip but that doesn't stop them from doing their gymnastic double act any time I try to get some shut-eye. It's impossible to sleep through that.'

Janessa laughed. 'Well...if you can't sleep, at least rest.'

'I do little else, my friend, whereas you look as though you're about ready to drop. Have you been burning the candle at both ends again?' At Janessa's shrug, Sheena eyed her friend closely. 'When was the last time you went out to the airfield?'

Janessa sighed. 'At least a fortnight ago. I didn't manage to get out last week.'

'Make sure you make some time, soon.' There was a caring note in Sheena's words. 'I need my Nessa in top form to look after my girls when they're born.'

Janessa placed her hand on Sheena's abdomen and

received a lovely fluttering kick in response. A smile came instantly to her lips. 'I'll be as bright as bright can be. Oh, I can't wait to meet them, Sheenie. I'm so excited.'

'Me, too. I know I whinge and moan but…' Tears glistened in her eyes and Janessa passed her a tissue. 'There I go again. My emotions are so unstable.'

'They're supposed to be,' Janessa dismissed with a smile, taking a tissue for herself and dabbing at her own eyes. She noticed that Sheena looked past her and realised it was probably one of the sisters coming in to take Sheena's obs. Glancing over her shoulder, she was stunned to see Miles Trevellion leaning against the doorjamb as though he'd been there for quite some time.

'Hey, Miles. Come on in. Janessa and I are just having a weeping fest. Care to join?'

'I'll give it a miss, but thanks for the offer.' He smiled at Sheena as he sauntered into the room and Janessa immediately put out a hand, grabbing hold of the end of Sheena's bed, in order to steady herself against the effect of his powerful smile.

He'd showered and changed out of his suit and in some ways she wished he hadn't. In a suit, he'd been just like all of the other consultants and surgeons she dealt with on a regular basis but now dressed in dark denim jeans that seemed to have long forgotten any shape but his own and a pale blue polo shirt, his dark brown wavy hair still a little damp from his shower, he was completely irresistible.

Up until now, the only dealings she'd had with Miles Trevellion had been when he'd been scowling or criticising her. Now…the smile that creased his face, the way his lips lifted to show off his white teeth, the intensity of his blue eyes as they sparked with life only enhanced his already naturally handsome features and, much to her chagrin, Janessa realised she wasn't as immune to him as she'd previously thought.

'H-How long have you been standing there?' she wanted to know, silently berating herself for stammering. She forced herself to look away from him, to concentrate on staring at the floor, but she found her gaze drifting back to his as he spoke.

'Long enough. I didn't want to interrupt your bonding moments. You two talk to each other in exactly the same way that my sisters talk to each other.'

'We feel like sisters,' Sheena answered.

'Is that so?' Miles raised his eyebrows as he walked slowly round to the opposite side of the bed from where Janessa stood. He was looking more at Janessa than at Sheena and quirked an eyebrow in her direction.

'We've known each other for years,' Janessa felt compelled to say, even though she wasn't sure why. It was just the way he was looking at her, as though he was accusing her of having too close a friendship with a person who was now a patient. Technically, though, Sheena wasn't her patient—the babies were.

'And neither of us actually *have* a sister,' Sheena pointed out, 'so we've ended up being the closest each other has.'

'Interesting.' Miles fixed Janessa with a curious stare. 'Does that mean it will be too much for you to look after the twins once they're born? You're emotionally involved with Sheena. What if something were to go wrong? Would you be able to cope with such an event?'

Janessa visibly bristled. 'Nothing is going to go wrong. That's why you're here, Dr Trevellion, and don't you dare think, even for one second, about removing me from this case. Whilst Sheena and I look upon and support each other like sisters, we are not biologically related, which doesn't make it at all inappropriate for me to care for her babies. Besides, our entire unit is like a close-knit family, so if you remove me from the case, you'll have to remove everyone, and that will benefit no one. There is nothing any of us, not only in the NICU but within Maternity and the other associated departments, wouldn't do for Sheena. She is beloved by us all and, in fact, I would go as far to say that *because* we all love her, the care we'll be providing for Ellie and Sarah once they're born and throughout their subsequent surgeries will be second to none.'

'Aw…' Sheena smiled at her friend, a fresh bout of tears gathering in her eyes. 'That was lovely. Thank you.' She reached for Janessa's hand and gave it a little squeeze, then turned to look at Miles, her voice firm but still personable. 'And you—don't you even dare think of moving me to a different hospital. I don't want to go to Philadelphia, even if they do have the highest success rate and experience with conjoined twins. These are my babies and I'll be having them right here, at Adelaide Mercy, with my extended family standing beside me, supporting me throughout the entire process. *I'm* the incubator and I have spoken.'

Miles looked from one woman to the other, his gaze settling on Janessa. She was standing proudly by her friend's bedside, her shoulders back, her chin raised, her eyes glinting with that defiance he'd witnessed earlier that day.

She looked…incredible.

After he'd left the NICU, he'd returned to Maternity and checked on Sheena before being directed to the hospital's residential wing, which was to be his home for the length of his stay. There was no point in trying to procure a furnished apartment close to the hospital as he'd be spending the majority of his time within hospital walls. Therefore, the one-bedroom apartment he'd been provided with was more than adequate for his needs.

He'd showered and changed his clothes, which had definitely helped him to wash away the long hours of travelling he'd had to endure. Once he'd unpacked, he'd headed out for a walk around the campus in order to get his bearings. The sooner he knew his way around the place, the better.

Throughout the entire afternoon, thoughts of Dr Janessa Austen had been niggling at the back of his mind, like an annoying noise he couldn't shut off. Twice, as he'd walked around, he'd seen a woman of her height and colouring and, thinking it might be her, had been astonished to find his heart rate increasing at the thought of enjoying another sparring match with her.

Then he'd wandered back to the NICU, in the hope of seeing her again, to get another look, to try and figure out exactly what it was about her that appeared to be intriguing him so much. When she hadn't been there, he'd politely asked one of the staff where she might be and had been told to check Maternity.

It was odd for his thoughts to be occupied in such a fashion, to be more than professionally curious about a colleague and now, as he stood opposite her, Sheena lying on the bed between them, Janessa Austen's rich brown eyes filled with determination, Miles finally realised the answer.

It was because she wasn't afraid to stand up for what she believed in.

It was clear that she believed in her staff, in her unit and in her bond with Sheena. She was a woman of substance and the more he spoke to her, the closer he was to figuring her out. Once he figured her out, he would be able to put her right out of his mind. He liked puzzles and the challenges they presented. That was no doubt the only reason *why* she'd even caught his attention in the first place. He was sure of it.

Miles slowly looked away from Janessa, his thoughts returning to the present. He smiled at Sheena, pleased she was still calm and controlled even though Janessa had become a little riled. 'Of course. You will stay at Adelaide Mercy. Dr Austen will be by your side, caring for your children every step of the way. Whatever you say goes, Sheena. You're the mother. You call the shots.'

'Good. Don't you forget it.' Sheena looked closely at Miles for a moment then grinned widely. 'You always were such a tease, Miles Trevellion. Always stirring. I see you haven't changed.'

'Why change perfection?' he asked, and gave a little bow. Janessa watched him and frowned again, confusion replacing her earlier annoyance.

'Stirring?' Janessa let go of Sheena's hand and placed both her hands on her hips. 'Do you mean that you were simply saying those things in order to get a rise out of me, Dr Trevellion?'

'You're in trouble now,' Sheena remarked to Miles in a sing-song voice.

'Not a rise, Dr Austen.'

'Then a test of some sort?'

'If you like.'

'You don't think that's a little juvenile? To test your new colleagues? Colleagues who, I might add, are all highly trained professionals?'

'Colleagues who have shown me that they're not afraid to stand up for what they believe in,' he countered. 'Colleagues who I now know are doing this job for more than the money they earn. There are two types of medical professionals in the world—those who do it for money and those who are called to serve their patients. I've worked with both over the years and in throwing a few bones at you, I've been able to see *how* you bite, *when* you bite and *why* you bite.'

'I hope you're not implying that Janessa is a dog in this scenario, Miles,' Sheena interjected laughingly. 'If so, don't go hiding behind me.'

Janessa couldn't believe what she was hearing, what her new and esteemed colleague was saying. He'd been testing her? Trying to rile her to see what sort of doctor she was? Anger, frustration and disbelief warred within her but there was also a part, deep down inside, that understood what he'd done.

He was a man who travelled the world, offering and applying his assistance to highly specialised cases, such as conjoined twins. He was a fount of knowledge and expertise, but as his placements would no doubt be of three to six months' duration it would mean he'd have to develop a foolproof way of sounding out his colleagues in order to know what type of personalities he was dealing with sooner rather than later.

She took another calming breath, crossing her arms over her chest, and met his look. 'Have you collated enough data on me, Dr Trevellion, or can I expect another round of your potshots?' Although her words were calm, her tone was cool.

The answer she received from him was a bright smile and where the last one had been aimed at Sheena, this one was definitely aimed directly at her...and she felt its full effect. Her mouth went dry, her heart rate instantly increased and she found her knees beginning to buckle. Without breaking eye contact, she gracefully sat back down in the chair she'd occupied earlier.

The man had straight, white teeth, a slightly crooked nose, a cleft in his perfectly square jaw, which was covered in a five o'clock shadow that only added to his air of powerful masculinity. All of that combined with his intense blue eyes, which now appeared to be filled with warmth and deep satisfaction, made a lethal combination.

'I'm very pleased to say that you've passed with flying colours, Dr Austen. Not only have you proved that you're willing to stand up for your staff and your unit, you've proved to be the perfect person to assist me in the care of Sheena's twin girls.'

'How magnanimous of you, Dr Trevellion.' She worked hard to keep her tone droll, as though she didn't care one iota about his opinion when in reality she did. Here was a man she'd looked up to in a professional capacity, reading his articles, interested in his research, delighted by his turn of phrase, and when she'd met him, she'd been disappointed to find him like so many other surgeons—overbearing and dictatorial. And then he'd walked into Sheena's room, smiling brightly, his eyes twinkling, his clothes fitting him to perfection.

Physically, he was gorgeous—and he no doubt knew it—but he was also showing her that he wasn't as unreasonable as she'd first concluded. Perhaps there *was* more depth, more substance to Miles Trevellion. Perhaps the man who had written those powerful articles, not only detailing the intricacies of neonate surgery but also somehow allowing his compassion for his little patients to bleed into the structure of his clinical articles, was making an appearance.

Sheena laughed at them both, her head turning from one to the other as though she were at a tennis match. 'Are you both seriously going to call each other Dr Austen and Dr Trevellion for the next six months? Seems a little old-fashioned and ludicrous to me,' she finished.

'Sheena's right.' Miles came around the bed and held out his hand to Janessa. 'I don't believe we've been properly introduced. I'm Miles.'

She stood, relieved when her legs appeared able to support her once more. Polite and professional. That was all she had to be towards him—polite and professional. 'Janessa,' she replied, and yet the instant his warm hand enveloped hers, she felt her logical thought processes fly out the window, and at the same time her knees started to buckle once more.

She stumbled a little and Miles instantly moved

closer, placing his other hand at her waist to steady her. His nearness only seemed to make things worse, as she breathed in his subtle spicy scent and became all too aware of just how close they were.

Gasping, she looked up into his eyes and was surprised to find him staring back at her, his blue eyes wide and slightly shocked. His eyes were perfect, so blue and so…perfect. Just like a sky on a cloudless day where she could take to the air and escape her life for a brief spell.

Her heart started to beat a little faster in her chest and her tongue came out to wet her lips. His gaze dipped for a second to witness the action, his Adam's apple sliding up and down his perfect throat. The world around them seemed to pause, just long enough that they could take a quick breath, drawing each other in before slowly exhaling.

'Janessa.' Her name sounded incredible spoken in his rich, deep tones and a wave of tingles spread throughout her body. This was wrong. It was ridiculous that she should feel an instant attraction towards this man when she wasn't even sure she liked him.

Naturally, she appreciated him as a colleague, easily accepting his genius in their chosen speciality and, of course, she'd fallen victim to a bit of hero-worship of such intelligence, devouring the articles he'd written the instant her editions of the *Journal of Neonatology* had arrived. That, however, didn't mean she needed to act like a silly schoolgirl simply because he was touching her.

Becoming cross with herself, she quickly disengaged any contact and spun away from him, taking two wobbly steps towards the door, her increased heart rate causing her breathing to remain uneven. 'Uh…anyway. I'd best go and…uh…check on a few of the babies before calling it a night.' She spoke quickly…too quickly.

'Are you all right?' Sheena asked. 'You're all flushed.'

'Am I?' Janessa raised a hand to her cheek and tried her best not to look at Miles but when she did, she saw him standing at the foot of the bed, his hands shoved into the pockets of his jeans. He was looking at her as though something strange had just happened but he wasn't exactly sure what. Had he felt it too? If so, what did that mean? Or perhaps this was another one of his tests. She quickly returned her attention to Sheena.

'Oh, that's probably because I've been up since four this morning. That's when our first new baby for the day decided to arrive and as I live the closest…well, I don't mind being called in.'

'Where do you live?' Miles asked, walking back to the other side of Sheena's bed, putting more distance between himself and his new colleague who, when he'd been close to her, had sent shock waves throughout his entire being such as he hadn't felt in an exceedingly long time.

He had no idea how or why this had happened, which was unusual for him. He was the man in charge, the one they all came to when they needed answers, and he liked it. The spark of awareness he'd just experienced when he'd been close to Janessa Austen meant absolutely nothing. He was a professional…and he was jet-lagged. Yes, that was most likely why this awareness of her had flared up. He was jet-lagged.

'Janessa's been living in the residential wing of the hospital for the past six months,' Sheena provided. 'She says it's the easiest way to keep an eye on me and the girls.'

He was surprised at this news. 'Really? Why not find an apartment close by?' Miles wanted to know, looking at Janessa who was almost ready to sprint out the door.

'Her house burned down and it's being rebuilt,' Sheena offered, answering for her once more. Janessa was glad of that as she was still struggling to get herself under control and to *not* look at Miles. 'We were supposed to go apartment-hunting but that's when I found out the twins were conjoined. I crumbled into a blathering mess and Janessa picked me up.' Sheena smiled lovingly at her friend.

'You'd have done the same for me,' Janessa replied, then opened the door, this time keeping her gaze trained on Sheena. 'Riley will be around soon to do his evening checks on you, but call me if you need anything, all right?'

'Yes, I'm fine. I have too many people fussing over me, especially Riley. What a fusspot of an obstetrician he is. Go. Sleep. See you in the morning.' Sheena waved to her friend.

Janessa nodded and with a polite smile aimed at Miles she all but ran from her friend's room.

The instant she was gone, Sheena turned to look at Miles, watching him closely. 'I don't believe it,' she said softly.

'Believe what?' he asked.

'You. Janessa.'

'What?' Miles was a little taken aback.

'Oh, don't play stupid with me. I've seen that look in your eyes before.'

'What look?' Miles settled down into the chair beside her bed and took her wrist in his fingers in order to check her pulse, hoping to distract her from whatever it was she was about to say. Fifteen seconds later, he released her. 'Good. How's your blood pressure?'

'Wendy.'

'Pardon?' Miles looked at Sheena.

'When we worked together ten years ago, we also worked with a doctor whose name was Wendy. Do you remember Wendy?'

'Of course I remember Wendy,' he replied a little briskly, and stood to walk to the end of her bed, unable to stay calm and seated if Sheena was determined to take him on a trip down memory lane. Wendy. How could he ever forget Wendy? He couldn't.

'You were very interested in Wendy when we met ten years ago.'

'What? How do you know?'

'You had this twinkle in your eyes. Every time she would come into the room, you would let your gaze rest on her a little longer than usual.'

'Are you sure you weren't projecting the way you used to stare at Will? Honestly, the two of you were madly in love. I still don't know why it didn't work out. He would never tell me.'

Sheena shook her head. 'We're not talking about me and Will, we're talking about you and Janessa.'

'Janessa?'

'Yes. You have the same twinkle in your eyes now as you did back then. You're interested in Janessa,' Sheena pointed out, then paused and tilted her head to the side, her tone a little softer. 'Whatever happened to Wendy? The two of you were such good friends back then but once my year was up I returned to Australia and sort of lost track of everyone.'

Miles looked down at his shoes for a second and then met Sheena's gaze. 'You were right in guessing I was interested in Wendy. I was, so much so that I married her.'

'What? You're married?'

'Widowed.' The word was spoken softly.

'Oh, Miles. Oh, I'm so sorry. I…I had no idea.'

He shook his head and touched her hand. 'It's fine. She died seven years ago in a train crash.' It was the night where his life had gone from wonderfully full to horrifically empty. 'I've had a lot of years to work through the different stages of grief.'

'That may be, but you're still alone, right?'

Miles nodded. 'It's not so bad. I have my work. I have strong bonds with colleagues.' He thought of his good friend Will Beckman and although he still wondered what had happened between Sheena and Will all those years ago, now was not the time to discuss it. There was no way he could risk a rise in Sheena's blood pressure simply to satisfy his curiosity. 'And now I get to hang out with you again so that's a bonus.' He smiled and watched as Sheena relaxed back against the pillows.

'And you get to work with Janessa, too. She's really quite amazing—don't let her youthful looks fool you.'

'Oh, I've already learned that lesson.' He shifted a little farther away from the bed and turned his attention to a large bunch of flowers on the shelf, pretending to be interested, hoping his words came out with the right amount of nonchalance. 'Janessa, while looking as though she's barely old enough to drive, has proved she's more than capable not only of running a hectic NICU but also of putting visiting consultants firmly in their place.'

Sheena laughed. 'That's our Nessa. And you like her.'

Miles breathed in deeply, the scent of the flowers reminding him of the sweet scent that surrounded Janessa, before slowly exhaling. 'I'm…interested,' he admitted.

Sheena clapped her hands and Miles couldn't help but smile as he looked at his friend. 'I knew it. The twinkle is unmistakable. So?'

'So…what?'

'So what are you going to do about it?'

'Nothing.'

'Nothing? Miles, how many women have you been interested in since Wendy died?'

He thought for a moment and then shrugged. 'A few, but nothing serious.'

'And I'll bet that none of them have captured your attention so completely and as quickly as Janessa, am I right?'

'Uh…' He shoved his hands into his pockets, feeling awkward. 'We don't need to discuss this, Sheena.'

'Hey. I'm the human incubator, who lies here day in, day out providing the best care a mother can for her babies, feeling as though I'm trapped in this room while the world keeps spinning without me. Throw me some crumbs, eh?'

Miles smiled at her words. 'All right, all right. I haven't pursued anyone since Wendy's death.'

'And now you're *interested* in Janessa?'

He exhaled harshly, his words tinged with a slight impatience. 'Do I like what I've seen of her? Yes. Am I intrigued to know more? Yes, but that doesn't necessarily mean I'm going to do anything about it.'

'What? Why not?'

'Because the life I lead is not suited to people like Janessa.'

'How do you know that? You hardly know her.'

'She has her world here. That's clear. She cares for her staff, her friends and most definitely for you, and my world is anywhere and everywhere. The fact that she's caught my attention is neither here nor there. I don't have the head space for any sort of romantic relationships.'

'Well, you at least be nice to her.'

'I will.'

'And take her out to dinner. She needs food. She's too skinny. But then again, maybe because I'm so fat and stuck in here all day like a beached whale, my perceptions are a little skewed.'

Miles laughed at her words but crossed to her side instantly, placing a reassuring hand on her arm. 'You're not fat.' His words were heartfelt. 'You're pregnant.'

'An incubator,' Sheena grumbled, but smiled back at him. Sighing, she looked at Miles. 'Janessa's special.'

'I'm beginning to realise that.'

It took the walk down the single flight of stairs to the NICU for Janessa's heart rate to return to a normal level as she tried not to replay every little minute detail of when she'd been dangerously close to Miles Trevellion.

He was turning out to be quite the chameleon. First he'd been brisk and arrogant, then supportive towards Sheena and then... And then what? Hot and heavy with her? No. The man had taken her hand in his purely as a form of greeting, and when her idiotic knees hadn't been able to cope with being so near to him, he'd placed a supportive hand at her waist in order to stop her from falling. He'd been caring and polite.

And what about the long and intense gaze they'd shared?

She closed her eyes for a brief moment, her heart rate once more picking up as she remembered the way he'd looked at her. Surprise, shock and sensuality. Until that moment, she hadn't thought it possible to get all three together but Miles Trevellion had pulled it off...with a bang.

Janessa shook her head, pushing the thoughts away completely. Work. Babies. Sheena. Sleep. Those were the important things in her life at the moment, not thoughts of Miles Trevellion, and with a deep breath she set off to do her job. After confirming that both Joey and Taneesha were doing just fine, and that the rest of the patients and staff were under control, Helena, who was on the night shift, shooed her away.

'You look completely worn out,' Helena said as she pointed to the NICU door. 'Food, shower and sleep. I'll see you in the morning.'

There was nothing else for Janessa to do than to head out of the NICU. She walked through the long corridors, the hospital catering team out in force as they collected all of the dinner trays from the various wards. Smelling the food reminded her she hadn't had much opportunity to eat today and as she headed outside beneath the sheltered walkway that led to the residential wing, her stomach grumbled. All she wanted was to get to her room, have some raisin toast and go to bed.

'Wow. I heard that. You must be really hungry,' a deep voice said from just behind her. Janessa didn't need to turn around to know who it was. She may have only known Miles Trevellion for less than a day but his voice was instantly recognisable. 'That's one growly stomach you have there, Janessa.'

It was strange to hear her first name coming from his lips, the deep rich tones somehow making her name sound sexy and sensual. He fell into step beside her. 'I guess it is.'

'Busy day?'

'How can you ask that? You saw first-hand what the NICU was like at lunchtime.'

'Yes, I did, and from what I can recall you handled everything beautifully. Especially impatient and demanding visiting consultants.'

She stopped walking and he stopped right beside her. Janessa looked up at him, wondering if this was another one of his tests or if he was being serious.

She searched his eyes, looking for a clue to help gauge his mood, and then immediately wished she hadn't.

His eyes were so blue, so bright, so clear, like the sky on a cloudless day, and even though the light outside was starting to fade, looking into Miles's eyes made her feel the same way she felt when she was up in her plane, soaring above the ground, without a care in the world. It was odd. No man had ever made her feel that way before. She sighed slowly and then closed her eyes, not wanting to be affected by him and cross with herself because it was clear that she was. He was her colleague and she had to remember that, to treat him with the same level of polite indifference she treated the other surgeons who slipped in and out of her unit.

When she opened her eyes, she made sure she didn't look at him directly in case she lost her train of thought again. 'What do you want, Miles? I'm off duty, I'm tired—'

'And you're hungry. I was thinking…dinner? I'm new in town and have no clue which restaurants are the good ones.'

She shrugged. 'You can get a list from Reception at the residential wing.' She started walking again, wanting to get back to the privacy of her own room so she could relax and unwind and forget all about

Miles Trevellion and the way he seemed to fill her entire body with tingles every time he looked at her.

'Actually, that was my attempt at asking you to join me. Sorry. Should have made that clear.'

Janessa stopped short and stared at him. 'You want to have dinner with me?'

'Yes. You're hungry. I'm hungry. I thought we could eat together. Clear the air a little.'

'If you're referring to the way you bawled out an agency nurse earlier to the effect that she's now requested never to return to the NICU again, consider the air cleared.'

'Good.' He shoved his hands in his pockets. 'Good. Well, now that the air is clear, I guess we can just have dinner and get to know each other better.'

'Why? You're a colleague and I—' She stopped arguing when her stomach growled again.

Miles decided enough was enough and gently put his hand beneath her elbow and directed them towards the taxi rank at the front of the hospital where he'd arrived that morning. 'It's just food, Janessa. I would like to sit across a table and eat food. I'd like to have some company while I do it and I also have some questions about the conjoined twins I'd like to ask you.'

'Oh. A business dinner.' She shrugged, easing away from his gentle touch, hoping the warmth currently spreading through her body would cease when she wasn't so close to him. She should turn him down, return to her room, eat her toast and sleep. That was what she needed to do and it would definitely put a bit of distance between them. However, she hadn't left the hospital grounds in over a week and the thought of having Giuseppe, the owner of her favourite Italian restaurant, cook her a huge plate of *fettuccini* made her mouth water. 'Do you like Italian food?' A taxi was driving by the road closest to the residential wing and she put her fingers in her mouth and gave a loud whistle. 'Taxi!' she yelled, and the car instantly drove up to the kerb.

Miles was stunned and pleasantly surprised at this turn of events. Who was this woman? She was well liked and respected by her peers, she was exceptional at her job, she was a caring friend to Sheena and now she was whistling loudly for a cab. Smiling, he opened the taxi door for her and as she slid inside he shook his head, even more delighted and intrigued by this amazing woman.

CHAPTER THREE

THE short taxi ride to her favourite Italian restaurant was completed with Janessa pointing out some of the immediate sights of Adelaide, which looked beautiful at dusk, just in case Miles asked her anything personal. She needed to keep reminding herself that this wasn't a date, it was just dinner with a colleague, and yet she was completely aware of him sitting so close beside her in the back seat of the taxi.

At the restaurant, they were warmly welcomed by Giuseppe and seated at a small table for two, their waiter lighting the candle in the centre of the table, giving the whole setting a more romantic atmosphere.

They read the menus, ordered and then sat looking at each other. Janessa tried not to fidget with the cutlery, telling herself again that this was not a date, just a dinner between colleagues to discuss Sheena's twins. At least if they were discussing work, there wouldn't be any of those long and awkward silences that often accompanied two people who didn't know

each other on a personal level. Awkward silences…
like…the one she was experiencing now.

'So…' Janessa cleared her throat, eager to get
this meeting off on the right foot. 'Uh…regarding
the girls, I know we'll be doing a lot of scans once
they've been delivered. However, what would happen
if it's discovered they share a femoral artery?'

Miles leaned back in his chair and considered her
for a moment. It was clear Janessa wanted to ensure
this *was* a business meeting and while he was still
highly intrigued by her, wanting to ask her more
personal questions, he'd play along for now.

'Well, my professional opinion is that we should
cross that bridge if we come to it.'

Janessa blinked, hiding a smile before trying
again. 'But what if there is a vein that's hidden,
that isn't picked up on the scans, and it gets severed
during the separation?'

'Then I suture it closed.' Miles leaned forward
onto the table, his gaze intent, his words earnest.
'Janessa, I know you're concerned about the upcoming surgeries for the girls, I understand how much
they mean to you, but nothing is going to go wrong.'
He shrugged. 'I'm here.'

She tried again. 'But what if—?'

'Janessa, there are too many variables to discuss
right now, right here, at dinner, especially with your

stomach grumbling and growling. We'll cover all eventualities and discuss every scenario in the coming weeks before the scheduled delivery of the twins. Right now, though, I'm hungry. You're hungry. Let's enjoy this meal.' He picked up his wineglass and took a sip. 'So…have you lived in Adelaide long?'

She blinked slowly at his obvious arrogance and the abrupt change of subject. 'But what if the girls—?'

'How long? One year? Ten years? Or have you always lived in Adelaide? It's not a difficult question, especially for someone as intelligent as you are.'

Janessa huffed and crossed her arms. 'Born and bred.'

'Travelled much?'

'We're here to discuss the twins, not talk about me.'

'I beg to differ. If you're going to be part of my team, I need to know a bit more about you.'

'And so discovering where I've lived helps you do that?'

'It gives me a sense of who you are and what's important to you. So…have you travelled much?'

'A bit.' She noticed that he seemed completely relaxed and at ease but, then again, a man as good looking and as intelligent as Miles would be quite used to meals like this. It was she who felt so odd, so naked and exposed.

'Would you like to do more travel?'

'Not at the moment. Especially with Sheena needing me.'

'Of course. It's clear that the two of you are very close.'

'Yes.'

He put his wineglass down and leaned forward, a bright smile on his face. 'Am I making you nervous?'

'A little.' The words were out of her mouth before she could stop them and she immediately closed her eyes in confusion as embarrassment washed over her. He was so smooth, so relaxed and charming. How was she supposed to keep herself under control when every time he looked at her he made her feel as though she was the only person in the world who mattered to him. She knew it was his *magnetism* that was drawing her closer with every word he spoke.

'You don't date much?'

The feeling of embarrassment instantly left her and her eyes snapped open. 'This isn't a date, Miles. It's a business dinner.'

'True. So, tell me about Sheena. How has she really been feeling? Sleeping much? What's her emotional status? As her friend, I'm sure you can give me a much clearer picture than what her chart and notes tell me.'

'True.' Relaxing a little, Janessa sipped her wine. 'She's…hanging in there. I guess that's the best way to describe it. Naturally, her emotions are like a roller-coaster ride, but that's to be expected. She's also scared, nervous, worried—again, just like any other mother-to-be. But I think she's also concerned about the publicity the babies will garner once they're born. I mean, I know and you know that conjoined twins happen more frequently than people realise—'

'One in every two hundred identical twin pregnancies is conjoined.'

'Exactly, and each one of them has their fair share of publicity, although thankfully nowadays the publicity is more centred on the health of the babies and the subsequent operations to separate them rather than the "freakish" angle. Still, Sheena's worried about that.'

Miles nodded. 'It's a natural concern and one I've dealt with in different ways depending on the different services of the hospital where the babies are born. I think, in this instance, with the way your NICU is set up, we'll be able to secure the girls in a private bay, with screens and curtains so they can still receive the specialist treatment they deserve.

Once they're stabilised, we can move them to a private paediatric ward, but that may not be for some months. It all depends on how healthy they are when they're born.'

'What about photographers and paparazzi? What about the other mothers in the NICU? What if one of them takes a photo of the babies and sells it to the newspapers? I'm not saying that any of them would, but I'm—'

'You're just trying to be prepared,' he finished for her, nodding. 'I completely understand. My suggestion is to take photographs of the girls within the first twenty-four hours, have your hospital PR people release them with an update on the girls' health and that should at least stop the temptation for people on the ward taking photographs and selling them.'

'Excellent idea. So clear, so straightforward, so simple. Brilliant.'

The waiter arrived with their entrées, the minestrone soup sending her gastronomic juices into overdrive. She grinned at Miles as she sipped the hot, tasty liquid, glad to finally be able to eat.

'When was the last time you ate today?'

'Um…' She swallowed her mouthful and broke off a piece of fresh, crusty bread which had also been brought to the table. 'Some time early this morning?

I'm not sure. I know I've had several cups of tea and coffee.'

'Some days are busier than others.'

'Some days I eat more than others.'

He nodded, knowing exactly what she was talking about. 'It all pans out in the end.' Miles lifted his wineglass, holding it out. Janessa picked hers up and chinked it with his. 'To finding time to have a meal,' he toasted, and she smiled, relaxing a little more.

As they ate, the conversation turned to different topics ranging from politics to health-care funding, to recent breakthroughs in medical science and back to Sheena and the twins. By the time they said goodnight to Giuseppe, thanking him for a splendid meal, and had caught a taxi back to the residential wing, Janessa's stomach was full and her guard had dropped.

She'd discovered tonight that the brilliant man who had written all the journal articles she liked was also interesting, charming and very funny. Quite a few times he'd made her laugh as he'd recounted antics from some of the experiences he'd had.

'As with all new parents, it's customary to name your children at birth,' he'd recounted. 'But with the second set of conjoined twins I was fortunate enough to assist with, the parents, who were from

Tarparnii, called their boys Ticanegia and Tocneshla. Then they shortened the names to Tic and Toc.' His smile had been bright, his eyes had twinkled with humour and Janessa had found herself just enjoying being with him as they'd laughed together.

He'd been a perfect gentleman, holding doors for her, insisting on paying for the meal and transportation, and now as they exited the taxi and headed for the residential wing, he walked close, his hand hovering in the small of her back as a means of protection and stability.

She swallowed as they walked into the reception area of the residential wing, feeling as though every eye in the place was on them.

'Evening, Janessa,' Arthur, the night-time receptionist-cum-security-guard, called, waving to her. 'And Dr Trevellion. Good to see you again.'

Miles guided Janessa over to the elderly but still fit man who had worked at this hospital far longer than either of them had been alive. Miles shook hands with the man, treating him with polite respect.

'Good to see you again, and please call me Miles.'

Arthur nodded, then asked, 'Did you manage to find somewhere good to eat?'

'Actually, I did. Janessa here was good enough to share her favourite restaurant with me.'

'Giuseppe's,' Janessa offered as she noticed

Arthur's bushy eyebrows rise in surprise. She could see that he was intrigued by the two of them being out together.

'It's good to see you getting out and about, young lady.' He turned his attention to Miles. 'She works too hard, this one.' He looked back at Janessa. 'You should get away from the hospital more often. Go for a drive in your fancy car.'

Miles's eyebrows rose at this information. 'You have a fancy car?'

Janessa shook her head, not wanting to talk about her car or the fact that it had belonged to her father. That car was part of her personal life and therefore had nothing to do with Miles Trevellion. 'It's just a car.'

'I like cars. A lot,' he offered.

She looked at him for a moment, tilting her head to the side in a considering manner. 'I'll bet you like to drive them fast, too.'

Miles's smile increased and he winked at her. 'You'd better believe it. Helps to keep the heart pumping. Makes me feel alive.'

Janessa was sure she should have said something, come up with a retort that he, as a member of the medical profession, should know all about the dangers involved in such daredevil behaviour, but her thought processes had turned to mush the instant he'd winked at her.

'Surely,' Miles continued when she didn't make any reply, 'you have ways of dealing with your stress? Tell me you escape from this place every once in a while and remember how to live life like a normal person, rather than a medical professional tied to their work?' When she still made no reply, he exhaled slowly. 'Life's too short, Janessa.'

'I keep telling her that,' Arthur agreed, and Janessa snapped out of her stupor, having forgotten for a moment exactly where she was. She straightened her shoulders as Arthur continued. 'I keep telling her to ease up a little.' He tut-tutted, his words spoken in a caring and familiar way.

'And I *will* ease up, once Sheena's babies are all healthy and well on their way to living normal lives.'

At the mention of Sheena, Arthur demanded an update and she was more than pleased to give it, especially as it meant she could stop fixating on how one simple wink from Miles had turned her into a dim-minded twit. 'These aren't just Sheena's babies,' he said to Miles. 'They belong to the whole hospital. Sheena's one of our own and here at Adelaide Mercy we take care of our own.'

Miles smiled. 'So I'm beginning to realise. It's great to work at a hospital that has such a close-knit community.' He looked at Janessa, remembering how she'd been firm and direct with him earlier on that day, protective of her staff, her NICU and her friends. He noticed that her eyelids were growing heavier and when she tried to stifle a yawn, rather unsuccessfully, he shook hands again with Arthur and led a tired Janessa towards the old lift.

'Which floor are you on?' Miles asked as he pressed the button to call the lift down.

'Three. Ordinarily I'd take the stairs but...' She yawned, then shook her head. 'This always happens. Now that I'm out of the hospital, it's as though my brain switches off and my body gives in to exhaustion.'

Miles nodded. 'Happens to me, too.' The lift arrived and he held the door for her, waiting politely while she went inside. He pressed the button for the third floor and they both waited while the old lift creaked its way upwards. 'Perhaps the stairs would have been safer,' Miles remarked cautiously as he looked around the old lift.

'Probably.' Fatigue was really starting to hit. She needed to get out of this lift, escape Miles Trevellion's enigmatic presence and settle down to a hopefully uninterrupted night. Even standing here with him, just the two of them, there was a strange awareness, being alone together in such a confined space, that seemed to surround them.

When the lift finally stopped, Miles once more held the door for her and Janessa thankfully stepped out into the hallway. She was about to turn and say goodbye when she realised he, too, had stepped from the lift.

'Are you staying on this floor as well?' she asked.

'Yes.' He dug into his pocket and pulled out a key. 'Apparently, the residential wing used to be the old nurses' home many moons ago.'

'Correct,' Janessa said as she made her way down the corridor.

'The third floor was where they converted some of the rooms into small apartments with a kitchenette and their own bathrooms, although I was told that the plumbing hasn't been all that crash hot lately.'

'True. I can ask for you to be moved to the first floor where they actually have a lovely two-bedroom apartment, complete with a proper sitting room and dining room. Much bigger. Nicer for you and the plumbing on that level is fine.' She wasn't sure she could deal with working *and* living so close to him. The fact that she'd been looking forward to his arrival and the realisation that the impatient doctor she'd met earlier in the morning was that of a man exhausted from international travel was now clearly evident. Since they'd headed out to dinner, he'd been nothing but kind, cordial and caring towards her. Still…living and working in such close proximity to him would make her far more aware of him than she already was.

'Thanks.' He stopped outside a door—the door that happened to be right next to the door Janessa stopped outside. 'But here will be fine for the next six months. I don't need that much room. Contrary to popular belief, I'm not one of those surgeons who is dictatorial and demanding.' He smiled at her and she noted the same teasing glint in his eyes that she'd seen when they'd been at the restaurant when he'd been relating some of his more humorous stories.

'Good to know,' she countered as she pulled out her key and inserted it into the lock.

He lifted his eyebrows in pleasant surprise. 'Neighbours, eh?'

'Looks that way. Hope you don't snore too loudly.'

He laughed, both of them standing there, looking at each other, the world around them disappearing. Even though she'd told herself all evening that their dinner hadn't been a date, she couldn't help but feel like he was about to kiss her goodnight.

Slowly, the smile slipped from his lips as they stood there, staring, the awkwardness mixing with the awareness that seemed to all but sizzle between them. Janessa looked up into his soothing blue eyes and found herself sighing, knowing that if she let herself go, she could look into his eyes all day long and never get bored. It had been a very long time since she'd been attracted to a man in such a way and the sensations he was evoking were making her feel all warm and tingly.

'Uh…' She swallowed over her dry throat. 'Well… thank you for dinner.'

'My pleasure. Thank you for coming with me. It was nice to spend my first evening here at Adelaide Mercy in such fine company.'

A shy smile touched her lips at his words. 'Oh… er…thanks, I guess.'

His rich, deep, chuckling laughter rumbled through her. 'Listen to us. So polite, so full of thank-yous.'

She nodded. 'Our mothers would be proud.'

'Yes. Yes, they would.' He shoved his hands into his pockets, unsure whether he should shake her hand, give her a polite hug or just nod and turn away. It was odd. He wasn't used to being unsure of himself.

'Well…' she said, uncertain what to do next. Her mind, which was usually fairly sharp, seemed to have shut down through sheer mental exhaustion… and the fact that he was so close to her.

'Well…' he repeated, knowing he should move, go

into his apartment and let her do the same. When she smothered another yawn, he nodded, decision made, and held out his hand in a polite form of saying goodnight. 'Get inside and get some sleep,' he said softly as she slipped her hand into his, pleased that he'd made the decision as to how they should end this evening. A handshake. Nice, polite, formal… maybe too formal. Perhaps a quick kiss on the cheek. Yes. A bit less formal, a bit more familiar but still professional.

She looked down at their hands, clasped firmly and perfectly together, the warmth from his touch spreading up her arm to burst forth and heat the rest of her insides.

At the slight tug on her hand, she looked up and realised, belatedly, that he was leaning towards her, heading in to kiss her cheek. However, the moment she moved her head, Miles's lips connected—not with her cheek but with *her lips*!

She gasped in shock and surprise but didn't immediately pull away, the world around them slipping and sliding and faltering a little as the pressure of Miles's mouth on hers remained intense, intoxicating and intriguing.

Her eyelids fluttered closed as his spicy scent wound its way around her, drawing her in, heightening every sensation now zinging throughout her. Pleasure, confusion, excitement, doubt.

He was kissing her!

She was kissing him!

Neither of them were moving away.

With her heart pounding so wildly against her chest, she thought it was going to break right through her ribs, Janessa stayed very still, scared that if she shifted, even slightly, he'd think she didn't like the sensation of having his mouth against hers.

Accidental? Yes. Powerful? Yes. Eager for more? Definitely yes.

He hadn't meant to kiss her, not like this, not on the lips, but she'd turned at the wrong moment and then…and now…and how was he ever supposed to think coherently ever again? He'd simply been intent on a firm and polite handshake, combined with a small peck on her cheek to let her know that he appreciated her going to dinner with him, and now it had turned into something unknown and electrifying.

He closed his eyes, either to memorise every moment they were sharing or to fight the urge to develop this impromptu kiss even further. The need to haul her close, to hold her firmly against him, to part her lips with his and—

Janessa jerked back, letting go of his hand and

stepping back against her apartment door. Miles opened his eyes and looked at her, unable to believe the repressed desire and complete confusion he saw reflected in her rich, chocolate depths.

'Goodnight.' The word was choked and dry against her throat. Quickly she turned her back to him, her heart still hammering wildly against her chest, her breathing erratic, her cheeks flushed and her legs threatening to fail her. She fumbled with her key but another second had her door open and she was soon safely on the other side of it.

Breathing a sigh of relief, glad she'd been able to break free from the overwhelming sensations Miles had evoked deep within her, she stayed where she was, head back against the door, eyes closed, eager for her lungs to once again be filled with the appropriate amount of oxygen.

'Goodnight, Janessa. Sleep well,' she heard him say through the paper-thin walls, and then she heard him open his own door and walk into his apartment. She closed her eyes again and allowed his rich, deep tones to wash over her, delighting at the way her name seemed to sound like a caress from his lips.

Slowly, she opened her eyes and pushed away from the door to walk on unsteady legs towards her bedroom. Miles had just kissed her! The man's lips had been pressed to hers and *she'd liked it*!

Flopping face down onto her bed, she whimpered in confusion. How on earth was she supposed to face him tomorrow at their nine-thirty meeting? How was she supposed to pull herself together and sit across the table from him and talk about work when all she would be able to think about was the way his mouth had felt so warm and perfect against her own?

She had no idea.

Miles put his key down on the empty bookshelf by the door and closed his eyes. Shaking his head, he couldn't believe what had just happened. He'd kissed another woman. Sheena had been right. He *was* interested in Janessa in the same way he'd been interested in Wendy. He'd loved and lost and the pain had nearly killed him. He couldn't...*wouldn't* go there again.

Whatever he felt for Janessa was irrelevant. He was there for the twins. All his relationships at Adelaide Mercy must remain professional. It was a matter of survival.

CHAPTER FOUR

JANESSA woke up upon hearing a noise and checked her alarm clock.

'Ten past three,' she muttered as she flopped back onto the pillow and sighed. With her eyes still closed, she fumbled around for her mobile phone and pager, which were on the nightstand next to her bed. Squinting, she looked with bleary eyes at the bright display on both of them but she hadn't received any messages or calls. Unsure what noise had woken her, she decided to ignore whatever it was and go back to sleep. Her alarm would be going off in just under three hours and after her hectic day yesterday she deserved all the sleep she could get.

Snuggling into the covers, she allowed her mind to settle back into dreamland where she'd been out at the airfield, flying in her plane, coming in to land, only to find someone was waiting for her. A man. A tall man. With dark brown hair and blue eyes, greeting her with a warm, welcoming smile. As she drew closer to the ground, she could see his features more clearly and was momentarily stunned to discover the man in question was none other than Miles Trevellion.

Her eyes snapped open at the realisation. She was dreaming about him? No. Ridiculous. He meant nothing to her. He was just a colleague...a colleague who had kissed her.

She moaned and buried her face in the pillow. Ever since the man had walked into her NICU, turning her world upside down, he'd been nothing but a harbinger of change and change was something she didn't like in her world. Change had brought her nothing but pain, trouble and, in the end, loneliness. First her baby, Connor, had died, then Bradley had left, her mother had died and later her father had become sick. She was fine if the change was initiated by her, that way she could control it, but Miles Trevellion was something she couldn't control and as such he posed a threat to her well-ordered life.

The only way to deal with this change was to treat him as nothing more than a professional colleague. The next time they met there would be no long stares, no touching and definitely no kissing.

She turned over, settling into a new position, forcing her mind to think of a different scenario to soothe her back to sleep.

She'd just started to settle, thinking about driving

her father's beloved Jaguar E-Cabriolet through the lush, green Adelaide hills, the top down on the car, the wind in her hair as all of her stresses floated away, when she heard a noise again. She instinctively knew it was the same noise that had initially woken her and it was coming from next door.

It was the beeping of Miles Trevellion's mobile phone, no doubt alerting him to the fact that he'd just received a text message. She huffed impatiently as she heard him move around next door, wanting him to be as silent as possible so that she could get some sleep. Didn't the man have any idea how thin these walls were?

Janessa waited for a few minutes, listening to him, trying to picture the way he'd be moving around the apartment she knew was the mirror image of her own. As she lay there, she began to wonder what he would be wearing. It didn't sound as though he had shoes on and he was obviously in the kitchen, making himself something to eat.

After another few minutes the noises seemed to settle and she once again started to relax, hoping he'd finished his pre-dawn snack and head back to bed. Then, in the next instant, his mobile phone rang, followed by the crash of a chair falling and then the kettle whistling to signify it had boiled.

'Oh, for heaven's sake,' she growled, and flipped

the bedcovers back. Stomping to the wall, she banged her fist on it. 'Can you keep it down, Miles? Some of us are trying to sleep.'

'Janessa?'

'Who else would you be waking at three o'clock in the morning?' she demanded.

'Sorry. Didn't realise you could hear me.' A pause then, 'No. No. Not you, Marta. Someone else—my neighbour.'

Marta? Janessa stepped back and looked at the wall in confusion. Through her sleep-deprived brain she belatedly realised he was talking on the phone to Marta von Hugen, who, she knew from the articles she'd read, was one of his colleagues in America.

Shaking her head, she stomped back to her bed and buried her face beneath the pillow, trying desperately to drown out the sounds from next door. She almost sky-rocketed through the ceiling, though, when someone knocked on her door. The pillow was tossed aside as she flicked back the covers and pulled a robe on over her short nightshirt. Usually, if there was an emergency in the NICU, she would be called or paged but sometimes they knocked on her door.

A second later she stood there, blonde hair loose and dishevelled, robe knotted at her waist, legs and feet bare, door open as she stared into Miles's wide-awake blue eyes.

'Didn't mean to wake you,' he began, 'but now that you're up, I was wondering if you have any herbal teas? I only have coffee,' he continued, 'which doesn't sit too well with jet lag.'

Janessa stood there, glaring at him, one hand on the door, the other over the knotted robe, ensuring that it didn't accidentally come undone. 'It's three o'clock in the morning, Miles.'

'I know, but we're both used to being woken at ridiculous hours and I really could do with that tea. One good strong cup of herbal tea will have me sleeping like a baby in no time.'

He smiled at her.

The combination of his eyes sparkling, his lips curving, his straight white teeth shining brightly at her caused her knees to tremble momentarily. Her hand tightened on the door, more for support than anything else. Damn, but he was good looking. She had to be strong. Resist his natural charm. She had to focus and be professional.

'I apologise once again for waking you and now for disturbing you,' he went on when she made no reply. 'My body clock is still on American time and I probably should have remembered to turn my phone to silent. If it's at all possible that you have some herbal tea, I just need one tea bag and then I'll be on my way, back next door, leaving you alone to go back to sleep. I promise.'

Again, Janessa didn't move, didn't say anything, just stared at him as though he was some sort of apparition. Was she still asleep? Sleepwalking? Sleep-pounding on the wall? Sleep-annoyed?

'One tea bag,' she finally murmured, before turning and walking towards the kitchen. As she hadn't actually invited him in, Miles stayed where he was, but by not following her he was treated to a wonderful view of her smooth, silky legs and the swish of her hips as she sashayed up the hallway. He swallowed, taking in the slim build beneath her silky robe, wondering exactly what she had on underneath.

He shook his head, trying to clear his mind. She was his colleague and the fact that he was clearly attracted to her was something he would need to fight. Then again, what red-blooded male wouldn't be attracted to Janessa Austen, especially when she looked so young and tousled, fresh from her bed, her hair all messed as it wildly framed the smooth skin of her face, her chocolate-brown eyes half-open and still sleepy? Certainly not him.

She returned a moment or two later, a box of herbal

tea in her hands. 'Take it. Keep it. The whole box. Drink as many as you need.'

'But I only need—'

'Take it,' she said clearly as she placed it in his hands. 'Consider it a welcoming gift.'

'Thank you, Janessa.' His smile was as bright as the early morning sun. 'That's very kind of you.' She could tell by the way he spoke and the look in his eyes that he was being sincere.

'It's not *that* kind, Miles. More like self-preservation.' Her words were still sleepy, tired and he could tell she was trying to hold on to that sensation where you were half awake and half asleep. It was common amongst doctors, especially when they had a callout. If there was any possibility at all of getting back to sleep, even for an extra twenty minutes, they clung to it. 'Now, if that's all, good-night…or morning…or whatever.' She yawned and covered her mouth with her hand.

'Yes. Of course. Sorry to have bothered you and woken you and generally annoyed you.'

'Uh-huh.' She was starting to close the door to her apartment, needing desperately to shut out the sight of him standing there, dressed in only a pair of jeans and a T-shirt that clearly outlined his firm, muscled torso. He was good looking, intelligent and far too appealing for this hour of the morning.

She was almost there, had almost managed to deal with the situation and close the door, desperately eager to get back to her bed, when her own phone started to ring.

'No. No. No,' she whimpered, closing her eyes and momentarily leaning her head against the open door.

'If it's an emergency, I don't mind going,' Miles offered. 'It's quite clear that you need your sleep, Janessa. Sheena told me that you've been working longer hours than usual of late.'

'I may as well give up on the whole sleeping thing,' she mumbled, leaving the door ajar as she headed back to her bedroom to answer the phone. 'Hello?' she said after connecting the call. She listened for a moment, closing her eyes. 'That's fine. I'll be right there.' She pressed the button on her mobile to end the call.

'Problem?' Miles asked and Janessa returned to the front door.

'It's Sheena. She's crying.'

'Crying? Why? What's wrong?' Miles was instantly alert.

'Nothing's wrong. She's just crying.' Janessa rubbed a hand over her eyes. 'Excuse me, Miles. I need to get dressed and go see her.'

'I'll go put shoes on,' he remarked, and before

she could say another word, he'd disappeared next door. Giving up, Janessa headed back into her room, dismissed the comfortable bed, which was calling her back, and quickly got dressed. Two minutes later there was another knock at her door and Janessa knew it would be Miles.

'Here,' he said as she opened her door, pocketing her keys, phone and pager. He held out a cup of what smelled like steaming black coffee. 'Black. Two sugars.'

'Coffee? How did you know how I drink it?'

He shrugged. 'I noticed at the restaurant. Anyway, I brewed some before I thought better of it and came to annoy you for some tea. I thought you could use a cup now, wake you up a bit more.' She was dressed in a pair of jeans and a baggy knit jumper, which looked warm and cosy. She'd brushed her hair, pulled it back into a ponytail and slipped her feet into a pair of flat shoes. She looked gorgeous, comfortable and very homely, and he realised that whether she was dressed as professional Janessa, sleep-tousled Janessa or comfortable, homely Janessa, she was an incredibly beautiful woman.

She wore no make-up and he detected no pretence about her. Miles couldn't believe how drawn he was to this woman. He'd worked with all different types of people over the years and ever since the death of his wife he'd been able to keep the lines between business and his personal life completely separate. Why couldn't he do it with her?

'Thank you. That was very thoughtful.' She gratefully accepted the cup and took a sip, trying not to be too affected by his kind gesture. She would have coped better with him being so close to her if he'd remained as lacking in charm and chivalry as she'd first thought, and of course before he'd kissed her. 'Mmm…just what the doctor ordered.'

Miles couldn't believe how pleased he was at her appreciation as they headed to the stairwell, both of them sipping the rich brown liquid as they went. 'You're more than welcome, especially after you gave me the whole box of tea.'

'What's a box of tea between friends?' she said as a throw-away line.

'Friends?' The word was spoken softly and with a hint of surprise. Janessa simply glanced at him over her shoulder and raised an eyebrow.

'You *do* know what friends are, don't you?'

Miles smiled, liking the teasing lilt in her tone. 'It's been so long, I'm not sure I remember how to make friends. I know how to deal with colleagues, patients, emergencies, but friends…?' He shook his head as they exited the stairwell, letting the sentence trail off.

'Well...' she drawled as they walked through the quiet residential wing foyer, Janessa waving to Arthur as they went by, 'it looks as though there's something to teach the great Miles Trevellion after all.' The words were delivered with a bright smile and Miles almost choked on the liquid in his mouth. He swallowed quickly and coughed once as he continued to stare at her.

In the artificial light of the hospital grounds, dressed casually, demeanour more relaxed than he'd previously seen, Janessa's smile was wide, bright and completely encompassing, her tired brown eyes twinkling with merriment.

'Good to know you're human, like the rest of us,' she added before they entered the hospital building and made their way to Maternity, several staff members greeting them with a quick hello or a polite smile and nod. Miles could tell that Janessa was not only well liked but respected and he was pleased that he'd be working alongside a colleague of her calibre.

He'd read dossiers on Janessa and other members of the Adelaide Mercy senior team who would be assisting with the various aspects of the twins' delivery and future surgeries. It was a policy of his to know as much about his teams as he could, and to know that Janessa not only had the skills but the caring personality to match this sort of work was definitely a bonus. Far too often he'd worked with surgeons and physicians who were only interested in the prestige and fame associated with something as unusual as separating conjoined twins. Thankfully, the team at Adelaide Mercy were all invested in this project and perhaps the main reason behind that was Sheena. She was one of their own, a staff member, a colleague, a friend—and even, as Janessa had declared, a sister.

Upon entering Sheena's room, Miles was once more able to witness the bond between the two women. Janessa crossed instantly to Sheena's side and put her coffee cup down on the bedside table before immediately embracing the bed-ridden woman, handing her a tissue at the same time.

'What's wrong?' Janessa asked in a soft, caring tone.

'Nothing,' Sheena blubbered. 'Everything. Oh, I don't know any more,' she wailed. Miles came and stood on the other side of the bed, watching, deciding it was best to step back and let Janessa handle this, given that she certainly knew Sheena a lot better than he did.

As Sheena continued to cry, apparently for no reason whatsoever, Janessa held her and stroked her hair, murmuring soothing noises until the tears began to stop. Miles couldn't help but notice that Janessa was very maternal, as well as so caring and patient. He wondered if she planned to have any children of her own in the future. Her dossier had stated that she wasn't married and, again, he was curious as to why not. She was only thirty-six years old, although she looked years younger, she was intelligent, funny and so incredibly beautiful. So why wasn't she already spoken for?

'There, now. Feel better?' she asked Sheena.

'No? Yes?' Sheena smiled through the final tears that Janessa was wiping away. 'I still don't know.'

'Pregnancy blues,' Janessa remarked, brushing hair from Sheena's eyes. 'That's all it was.'

'I was lying here and I started thinking about everything, about things that could go wrong, about the surgeries, about how on earth I was going to cope…'

'Doubts and concerns are very natural,' Miles said, and Sheena quickly turned her head, surprised to find him there.

'Miles? I didn't see you come in.'

'He came with me,' Janessa said.

'With you?' Sheena wiggled up the bed and stared at them both.

'Not *with me* with me, it's just that Miles woke me up and then needed tea and then after the phone call, he made me coffee and as we were both awake we, uh…came together. Not *together* together but…' Janessa fumbled over her words and started to blush as she realised the more she explained, the more incriminating it sounded.

'I'm staying in the residential wing, next door to Janessa,' Miles interjected, his tone smooth and commanding. 'I'm still jet-lagged and was receiving phone calls from overseas. My phone woke Janessa. It's all very simple and quite innocent.'

'Exactly,' Janessa said, not wanting to talk about it further, given that Sheena had a knack of seeing straight through her emotions. 'Now…back to you. Do you want to talk about some of these concerns?'

'They're the same ones I've had all along.'

'Well, now that Miles is here, perhaps if we go through them again, he'll be able to give more in-formation.'

'Good idea.' Miles came back round the bed to the same side as Janessa, pulling out a chair for her before getting one for himself. Settling down, he fin-ished his coffee and looked expectantly at Sheena. 'I'm here to help.'

'Uh… OK. Let me see…where to begin.'

Janessa could see Sheena was trying to get her mind in gear. 'Let's start at the beginning. With the birth. From what Riley—Sheena's obstetrician,'

Janessa added in case Miles hadn't met Riley yet, 'has said, there's no question of a natural birth and that is why the C-section has been booked for two weeks' time.'

'That's right.' Miles nodded. 'With the growth hormones we're administering to the twins each day, this should help their bodies to develop a little faster than usual. There's a chance, as they're sharing the same placenta, that one is being more nourished than the other. However, after taking a good look at the data gathered on the twins so far, it appears that this is well under control. The stronger they are when they're born, the better chance they have when it's time to perform the first of the surgeries.'

'And the delivery? Riley said it's a straightforward procedure. Is that really true?' Sheena wanted to know. 'I've been there for plenty of deliveries before, I know what it's like, but I still keep thinking that so many things could go wrong.'

'They can, and you're right to be concerned. In some ways, because you're highly trained in the medical field, this can be seen as a disadvantage. You *know* what can go wrong and so you may tend to fixate on that. However, you have to trust this team.'

'Miles is right,' Janessa added. 'Riley is a brilliant obstetrician and you've worked with him long enough to know that he's able to think fast and clearly on his feet.'

'True.' Sheena sighed and nodded. 'So the actual birth of the girls is the easy part?'

'Precisely. Depending on their status at twenty-four hours, nothing will be done for the first few days, unless it's absolutely necessary. We'll be taking in-depth radiographs and CT scans of the girls but these will be done while they're mildly sedated.'

'And when will the first lot of surgeries commence?' Sheena yawned and Janessa could see that in discussing these issues with Miles, Sheena's mind was starting to let go of some of her concerns. This was good. What Miles was saying to her, keeping everything straight forward, honest and simple, was exactly what Sheena needed to hear. Keeping Sheena calm meant that her blood pressure would stay under control. If it shot up, they would need to perform the Caesarean sooner.

'There's no exact time frame for the surgeries as it all depends on the health of the girls. One set of twins I worked with weren't finally separated until they were almost two years old. Each set is unique and, as such, needs to be treated in the same manner.'

'OK.' Sheena closed her eyes and Janessa stood.

'That's enough for now. I know you have more questions for Miles, but he's not going anywhere so don't stress.'

'Good idea.' Sheena yawned and slowly opened her heavy eyelids. 'Thank you. Both of you.'

'You're more than welcome,' Miles stated, moving the chairs he and Janessa had been sitting on out of the way. 'We'll see you in a few hours' time.' He leaned over and squeezed Sheena's hand. Janessa couldn't help but be impressed by him. He really did care.

As they tiptoed out of Sheena's room, heading towards the nurses' station, Janessa turned to face him. 'Thank you.'

'For?'

'Putting her mind at rest. Not giving her platitudes. Being supportive.'

'The same could be said of you.'

'Yes, but I'm her friend.'

'So am I.'

'Ahh…so you *do* have friends,' Janessa teased, a small smile on her lips. 'Good to know.'

Miles returned her smile. 'Amusing.' His tone was droll but the look in his eyes let her know they were on the same wavelength. The realisation stunned her. The same wavelength? First she was attracted to the man and now she was connecting with him?

The smile slid slowly from her face and she swallowed over the realisation. Distance. She needed to find a way to distance herself from him, to stay professional but still be polite and friendly.

'So…are you ready to head back to bed?' The words out of his mouth were warm, deep and husky and Janessa felt a blush instantly come to her cheeks, especially when the night sister, who was sitting at her desk, gasped in surprise.

'Uh…he doesn't mean… We're not…' Janessa began, but stopped. She closed her eyes for a second, then took a calming breath. When she opened her eyes, she was determined not to be so flustered by the man who was now regarding her with keen interest, obviously waiting to see what she would say.

'Dr Trevellion and I are both staying in the residential wing,' she informed Sister. 'Not together…' She shook her head. 'He's in one apartment. I'm in another.'

'We're neighbours,' Miles added, as though trying to help her out. 'But the walls between our apartments are so thin we may as well be living together.'

Night Sister nodded politely, but the wide smile on her face said she was still highly interested in the dynamic that seemed to clearly exist between the two neonatologists.

Janessa groaned and shook her head. 'You're no

help at all,' she muttered, before heading from the ward. She didn't wait for him and he didn't catch her up. For all she cared, he and his wide-awake, jet-lagged mind could stay in the hospital and do whatever he wanted. She still had a couple of hours before her alarm went off and she was going to get some sleep, even if it meant wearing earplugs in order to drown out the noises of Miles on the other side of the paper-thin walls!

You may be able to drown out the noises he makes, the little voice in the back of her mind told her, *but there's no way you'll be able to stop thinking about him.*

CHAPTER FIVE

JANESSA jolted instantly awake when the sound of an alarm clock buzzed all around her.

'What?' She sat bolt upright, the journal she'd been reading to help her get back to sleep flying across the room. She reached out a hand to turn off her alarm clock, but to her astonishment found that the sound wouldn't stop.

'What?' she said again, her brow puckering in tired confusion. She rubbed her bleary eyes and focused more clearly on the clock: 5:59 a.m. As she stared at the numbers, they changed to read six o'clock and with it came the sounds of the morning radio show she usually woke up to. The buzzing, however, still persisted and she stumbled out of bed, trying to figure out if it was a fire alarm or an evacuation alarm. Should she be grabbing her clothes and important case notes and rushing from the building?

Janessa walked bleary-eyed around the apartment, following the sound of the buzzing, now desperate to track its origin so she could stop it. She walked towards the kitchenette and it was only then that she realised the buzzing was coming from next door. From *Miles's* apartment. Did the man have it in for her? Was he intent on disturbing her any way he could?

She stared at the wall. 'You have got to be kidding me!' What was he doing? Why wasn't he turning it off?

Tired and still a little groggy, she pounded on the wall. 'Miles!' she called. No reply. Concern started to prick at the rear of her mind. 'Miles?' she called again, pounding a little louder on the wall. 'Are you in there?'

'Huh? What?' His sleepy voice, all rich and deep and completely yummy, came through the wall. 'Whaddya want?' he called again, and this time his tone was slightly muffled and impatient, as though he'd put a pillow over his head in order to block out the noise.

'Turn your alarm off,' Janessa yelled, starting to feel silly talking to a wall. She crossed her arms over her nightshirt, her feet now starting to get cold as she hadn't put on her slippers.

'What? Janessa?'

The way he said her name, all dazed and confused and sexily sleepy, made her close her eyes as a wave of comfortable warmth washed over her. When she'd returned to her apartment, she'd still had a bit of trouble getting to sleep, thoughts of Miles and his gorgeous smile, his hypnotic eyes, his firm, con-toured body keeping her awake.

Now, to hear him mumble her name as though he couldn't quite figure out exactly where she was but wanted her to come closer, it only made her aware-ness of him escalate. In order to get back to sleep she'd picked up the latest copy of the neonate journal she subscribed to and begun reading…until she'd come across an article written by Miles Trevellion.

She'd felt a little strange, reading the words written by the man who only last night had kissed her! She closed her eyes, reliving the sensations, astonished at her own reaction. Why hadn't she pulled away sooner? Why hadn't he? It was the first time in such a very long time that she'd been kissed by a man in such a way and while she knew she shouldn't, given that he was a colleague, she wanted more.

More kissing, more touching, more talking, more being with him. It was silly and schoolgirlish but she couldn't help the way she felt. Thoughts of Miles Trevellion had been constantly on her mind since he'd walked into her NICU. Janessa thought back to the way he'd been at dinner, respecting that she'd wanted to keep things on a more professional level but excited when he'd shared some of his thoughts with her about the research he'd undertaken. He'd made her feel smart and worthy of his attention. It had been nice.

When she'd heard him return next door, she'd sighed, listening to him move around in his apartment. He'd started whistling softly to himself and Janessa had lowered the journal and closed her eyes, deciding to enjoy the sweet sound. Relaxing more, she'd eventually drifted off to sleep where visions of the man had infiltrated her dreams…nice dreams… dreams in which he was smiling down into her up-turned face, holding her close and pressing his lips to hers as though he thought her the most precious and gorgeous woman in the world.

And then the buzzing had started…the buzzing that was still going.

'Turn the alarm off, Miles,' she called through the wall.

'Janessa?' Again her name from his lips was one of deep confusion, as though he wasn't quite sure where she was.

'You woke me up. Again!' she accused, shaking her head and opening her eyes. It was better for her to be standoffish with him, to keep him at a professional arm's length because if she allowed thoughts of him to intrude into her already over-burdened mind, things could get sticky. Yes, he was brilliant;

yes, she enjoyed being with him; yes, she couldn't help but fantasise about him pressing his lips to hers again and again—but the simple fact was that Miles was her colleague and one who would leave in six months' time.

She thumped once more on the wall. 'Turn it off,' she called, and stomped over to the sink where she filled the kettle and switched it on. She needed tea, preferably one of the calming, herbal varieties, in order to get her mind back to a more neutral place. It wasn't until she opened the cupboard that she remembered she'd given him the whole box of tea earlier that morning.

Closing the cupboard, she couldn't help but growl, her frustration increasing. The man really was impinging on her life. She had to keep things polite and impersonal. She was expected in the unit in an hour's time and she had hoped to get through quite a bit of paperwork before then. It looked as though this was yet another day in her life that wasn't going to plan.

Sighing heavily, she put two pieces of raisin bread into the toaster and settled on having a glass of juice, pottering around in her kitchen until finally the buzzing of Miles's alarm eventually stopped.

'Thank you!' Her words were called loudly, tinged

with impatience. The man was disturbing her enough *without* his alarm clock joining in the fun.

'Sorry. Didn't want to oversleep. Forgot where I was,' he returned, and his words made Janessa feel a little contrite at having been so annoyed with him. She didn't envy him the jet lag at all.

'It's fine.' All she wanted now was for him to keep quiet so she could get her head back on track and get ready for the day ahead. A quick breakfast, a quick shower, then dress, collect her paperwork and head to the unit. As she pulled out a plate and knife from the cupboard, waiting impatiently for the toaster, she almost jumped when Miles spoke again.

'Were you able to get back to sleep all right, Janessa?'

This time, though, he wasn't yelling through the wall. He was speaking quite normally and she actually looked around behind her to check that he hadn't somehow wondered into her apartment.

'Yes,' she answered hesitantly.

'That's good. These walls really are quite thin, aren't they?'

'Yes.'

'This is so odd. It's as though if I were to punch my fist through this plasterboard I'd be able to see you.'

'Don't do that,' she called urgently, looking at the

part of her kitchenette wall where his voice was strongest. If he did that, he'd see her dressed in her thin nightshirt and bare feet. Even the thought of him looking at her now made her cheeks tinge with colour. 'Uh…it would take for ever to get someone to come and fix it,' she added, trying to cover over the embarrassment she felt. 'Besides, you'd no doubt do an injury to your hand and we can't have those surgeon's hands damaged, now, can we?'

His answer was a rich, deep chuckle. 'No. We can't have that.'

The toast popped up but Janessa didn't move. She was glued to the spot, staring at her blank wall where she was sure he stood. He really was so close and yet so far. She walked to the wall and placed her hand against it, almost wondering if she'd feel the heat radiating from his body, but that was plain ridiculous.

'No. What's ridiculous is the way you can't seem to stop thinking about him, the way you hang on his every word and the way you're letting him affect you,' she murmured to herself.

'Did you say something?' he asked.

'Uh…' She moved away from the wall and backed out of the kitchenette. 'I'm going to have a shower,' she remarked, deciding to eat later at the hospital rather than staying in the apartment any longer than she had to. She couldn't believe how aware she was of a man she'd only just met and one she barely knew at all.

As she turned on the taps in the shower, the pipes groaned and creaked and moaned before the water spluttered out in nothing but a trickle. 'Ugh. Not now.'

She felt highly self-conscious of the fact that Miles could hear every little move she made. Why she should feel so…self-conscious about it all she wasn't quite sure. It was illogical to think he would smash a hole through the wall and if she'd learned anything about him both through his journal articles and the ridiculous tests he'd put her through yesterday, it was that Miles Trevellion was a logical man.

As she waited for the water pressure to increase, she still felt as though he could see through the walls, could see her standing naked in her shower, and the thoughts made her entire body flush with sensual embarrassment. What on earth was wrong with her? Usually, she could disregard any feelings of awareness she felt towards colleagues, preferring to admire them in a professional capacity. So why was she unable to do it with Miles? What was so different about him?

Until yesterday, when they'd met, her life had had a steady rhythm. Sleep, work. Sleep, work. The oc-

casional day off where she would go to the airfield,
fly in her plane and release her stress. Now Miles
was in her life and he seemed to bring a different
beat, a different rhythm to her world, one that made
her heart go *pit-a-pat* with excited awareness and
she wasn't quite sure what she should do about it.

Sighing, she turned off the taps and dried herself,
knowing the sooner she headed to the NICU, the
better off she'd be. Space. Distance. Separation. That
was what she needed from her new neighbour and
colleague, and the sooner the better.

Janessa quickly dressed in a pair of dark blue trousers and a pale pink knit top. Her hair was pulled
back into her usual ponytail, out of the way and easy
to put up into a surgical cap if necessary. Slipping
her feet into flat, comfortable shoes, she quickly
tidied her kitchenette and picked up the papers she'd
brought over from her office the previous night.

She was about to walk out the door when she heard
the squeak of the taps being turned on next door
and the pipes shuddering as though they resented
the fact that they had work to do. Janessa stopped,
holding her breath as she unashamedly listened to
the sounds from next door. Miles was in the shower.
The water was running and she swallowed, closing
her eyes, the picture of him standing with water
dripping down around his brown hair, his angular

face, his broad shoulders before sliding sensually over his firm torso and then down—

Her eyes snapped open and she swallowed over her thoughts. This was wrong. Him being so close to her was wrong. Miles and his enigmatic presence, his deep voice, his sexy body, his heart-stopping grin. She was a doctor, for crying out loud. The human body was just that to her—a body—and the fact that Miles Trevellion seemed to have a very nice specimen was of no concern. None whatsoever. Shaking her head, she grabbed her keys and opened her door. The sooner she was out of there the better.

And then he started to sing. Janessa paused, her hand curling tightly around her keys as she listened. He had a lovely voice. His smooth baritone made easy work of the notes and as she forced herself to move forward, closing her apartment door behind her, she found she was humming the same song as she headed down the stairs. Darn Miles. How had he managed to get so stuck inside her head so quickly?

She liked her space and Miles seemed to have infiltrated it at almost every turn. With Sheena, with the NICU and with her accommodation. Well…at least she still had her flying to herself. Escaping from the world and flying in her plane on her days off was by far her most favourite thing to do. Not only did it remind her of great times she'd spent with her father but also whisked her away from the pressures of hospital life. She hadn't managed to get away enough lately but now, with the latest stressful addition to her little world, she was looking forward to heading out to the small airfield as soon as possible.

'Morning, Janessa,' Ray said brightly as she walked into the ward half an hour after Miles's alarm clock had woken her up. 'I was just about to make coffee. Can I get you one?'

She nodded, her stomach growling due to her aborted breakfast. She didn't want to think about it because that meant she'd have to think of the cause of her aborted breakfast and she'd already thought way too much about Miles Trevellion this morning. 'Thanks, Ray. How was last night?'

'Helena's handover recounted a non-eventful night. You've just missed her.' He headed to the unit's kitchenette and pulled out two cups before using the small espresso machine which had been a gift to them all from very grateful parents.

'Taneesha's stable? Joey didn't turn blue again?'

'Everything's fine. A good night—which was a godsend, given how full the unit is.'

'Still, there are quite a few babies who can be transferred to Maternity to be with their mothers today, so that should give us a bit of wriggle room.'

'Great.' As Ray made their drinks, he gave her a few more details about the handover from Helena, knowing that as soon as they'd had their coffee, they could do a quick round and make firmer decisions regarding the precious little ones in their care.

Ray handed her a cup that had a big red love-heart on the side and the words 'Fill my Heart' written beneath it, and for some reason she immediately thought of Miles. Janessa shook her head as though to clear it before sipping at the liquid with grateful thanks, deciding she really didn't want anyone to 'fill her heart' and that she was more than happy to keep her life exactly the way it was.

The awareness she felt towards Miles Trevellion was nothing but a reaction to being out of the dating game. Besides, she wasn't looking for any sort of romance in her life, especially not with a man who would be leaving Adelaide Mercy in six months' time.

As she walked to her office to read over the notes and reports from last night, sipping her coffee as she went, she told herself to be satisfied with everything she had. She was head of the NICU, a job she'd worked long and hard to achieve. The people she worked with on a daily basis were some of her closest and dearest friends. They'd supported her through her father's cancer treatments, had been there for her when he'd decided he was through with fighting the debilitating disease and had passed away.

They were a family. Kaycee and Ray and Helena and Sheena. Arthur was over in the residential wing, always looking out for her, just as her father would. There was also the staff on the maternity ward and Charisma, the hospital director who was an advocate for the right person in the right job. Janessa may not have any blood relatives, she may be all alone in the world as far as biological family went, but here, at Adelaide Mercy, she had her *real* family and she didn't need anything more…especially not romantic or sensual thoughts about Miles.

So the man had kissed her. It didn't mean anything. He'd simply meant to kiss her cheek in a polite gesture of thanks for a nice evening. The fact that their lips had met meant nothing…nothing at all.

With her mind firmly back on track, she was able to focus on her work. She had a meeting about Sheena's conjoined twins at nine-thirty, and headed to the maternity ward to say good morning to her friend just after nine. By this time the breakfasts would have been served, the ward rounds would have been done and Sheena would no doubt be ready for a soothing cup of herbal tea.

Janessa stopped off at the maternity kitchenette,

made two cups and headed towards Sheena's room, calling various hellos to the staff as she went. She was humming happily as she nudged the door open to Sheena's room.

'Hi. Sorry I'm a little later than usual, this morning,' she said, her hands full with the two drinks. As she turned and looked towards her friend's bed, she was startled to see Miles Trevellion sitting in a chair by Sheena's bed.

'Oh. Hi. Sorry. I thought you'd be free.'

'Miles was humming that same song when he came in this morning,' Sheena pointed out.

Janessa looked at Miles, feeling like a deer caught in the headlights. The fact that she was humming the same song as him meant he knew she'd heard him singing it in the shower earlier that morning and for a split second it was as though the two of them were transported to another world, away from the hospital room, away from Maternity—back to when they'd been having a conversation that morning, only plasterboard and paint between them. Intimate. Indulgent and completely insupportable. She simply had to stop her mind from contemplating her new colleague in such a fashion.

'We both must have heard the same song on the radio,' Miles eventually murmured, his lips curving into a small smile that told Janessa that he knew exactly where she'd heard that song this morning and it hadn't been the radio.

Sheena held out her hands for the cup of tea. 'Ah, thanks for the tea,' she remarked, seemingly oblivious to the undercurrents passing between Janessa and Miles. 'I've been waiting for an eternity. I was starting to become quite desperate for my morning Janessa cuppa-tea-time.'

Janessa smiled at her friend, blatantly doing her best to ignore the tall, dark and sexy man in the room. 'I see the exaggeration hormones are working well this morning,' Janessa remarked.

Sheena laughed, but sipped the tea as Janessa put her cup down on the bedside locker, knowing that if she didn't she might drop it. She could feel Miles's gaze on her, watching everything she did, taking in the camaraderie between the two women. It was quite astonishing that he had such an ability to unsettle her, especially as she hadn't even known him for twenty-four hours.

Janessa pulled up a chair on the other side of the bed from him and looked at her friend. 'Did you keep sleeping after we left?'

'On and off, but no more waterworks, thank goodness,' Sheena admitted with aplomb.

'You told me you'd managed to sleep well,' Miles immediately interjected with instant indignation.

Sheena sighed. 'Yes, but I can lie to you. I can't lie to Janessa. She knows me far too well for me to get away with it.'

Janessa picked up her tea and hid her smile at Miles's reaction behind her cup. 'But Sheenie, you shouldn't lie to any of us,' she said after a moment. 'You don't like it when your patients lie to you,' she pointed out calmly.

'My patients *can't* lie to me. In fact, nine times out of ten they can't even talk, given that they're babies and young toddlers,' Sheena felt compelled to point out, but looked from Janessa to Miles. 'Oh, all right,' she grumbled. 'I won't lie to Miles any more, and it wasn't technically a lie, more like a nice exaggeration of the truth.'

'Thank you.' Miles nodded, seemingly satisfied, then turned to Janessa. 'Would you like to examine Sheena?'

Janessa shook her head. 'I'm sure between you and Riley, Sheena and the girls are well cared for. Besides, the nurses keep me up to date with anything out of the ordinary. We've got a good team here.' She sipped at her tea. 'I'm just here for a chat before our morning meeting.'

'Yes, and it's a meeting,' Sheena remarked indignantly, 'that I'm not allowed to attend, even though it's about me and my girls.'

'You're not the doctor, remember. You *are* the important incubator.' Janessa's words were not unkind but spoken with utter respect. She held out her tea cup and the two women chinked their mugs together. 'No one else can do your job.'

Sheena scoffed at that. 'Ha! Job? I lie here and do absolutely diddly-squat.'

'And that's the most difficult job of all,' Janessa agreed. 'See? We keep the tough jobs for those who can handle them.'

'Yes,' Miles agreed. 'It's important for your blood pressure to remain constant and as such…' he waggled a finger at her '…no cajoling the staff for information about patients.'

Sheena grimaced. 'It wouldn't work even if I wanted it to. Janessa's put a gag order in place.'

'A gag order?' Miles looked from Janessa to Sheena.

'I'm not allowed to know the ins and outs of what's happening in the wards because if I knew I'd get all bothered and impatient and want to go and help.'

'Really?' His eyebrows were raised in surprise.

'I know.' Sheena rolled her eyes. 'Can you believe it?'

Miles met Janessa's brown gaze and smiled, nodding slowly. 'An excellent idea, Janessa. Gag order. I've never heard it called that before. Well done.'

Janessa raised her eyebrows in surprise at the compliment. 'Er…thank you?'

'It's good to see that you're not only looking out for your friend in a personal capacity but in a way most doctors wouldn't have even thought necessary.' He stood from his chair and straightened his jacket, buttoning it up. 'I give credit where credit is due.'

'Nice to know,' she murmured, only glancing once or twice in his direction. If she looked at him, really looked across and met the deep blue of his eyes, she wasn't sure she'd have the strength to look away, especially given how gorgeous he looked in that suit.

There was a silence in the room for a second and an uncomfortable one at that, with the awareness she had of her new colleague. She sipped her tea, glad of something to do. As the room clock ticked on for another ten seconds, Miles eventually cleared his throat and addressed his comments to Sheena.

'I'll come by later and check on you again. Better go get ready for that meeting.'

'OK. Thanks for visiting,' Sheena replied as he headed around the bed and walked towards the door.

'Janessa, I'll see you at the meeting,' he remarked.

'Yes. See you there,' she sort of threw over her shoulder, looking vaguely in his direction. When he was gone, Janessa visibly relaxed in her chair, closing her eyes for a moment, only to encounter

Sheena's interested stare when she finally looked at her friend.

'What was *that* all about?' Sheena asked with astonishment.

'What?'

'You and Miles. Honestly, you could cut the air with a scalpel the tension between the two of you is so palpable.'

'I have no idea what you're talking about.' Janessa feigned innocence and continued drinking her tea.

'Oh, seriously? There were sparks flying between the two of you from the instant you entered this room.'

'Sparks?'

'Janessa. He's not like Bradley. Miles has been through things and, unlike Bradley, he'll stick around. I know you were devastated that Bradley wasn't there for you, to be with you as you both grieved for Connor's loss, but not all men are like that.'

'All men? Meaning Miles?'

'He's a great guy, Nessa. Strong and dependable. You two are good together.'

'Together? No. We're not together.' At her words, Sheena gave her a disbelieving look. 'You think there's something going on between Miles and myself, don't you?'

'Is there?'

'Yes.'

At this word, Sheena sucked in a breath and clenched her hands at her chest, excitement in her eyes.

'It's you. *You* are why we're here, why our worlds have connected. We are both here, working together because of your girls. They deserve the best care in the world and that, if I may be so bold, is Miles and myself. So technically, Sheenie, it's all *you*. There are no sparks, no tension. Just real honest concern for you and your girls.'

'Now you've made me disappointed.' Sheena dropped her hands back to her rub her belly. 'Hear that, girls? Aunty Janessa is trying to fool herself into thinking that she's not attracted to Uncle Miles.'

'*Uncle* Miles? When did he get promoted to uncle status?' Janessa wanted to know, feeling mildly indignant that he should get the same level of honorary title as herself, and yet Sheena didn't know him nearly as well. She finished her drink and stood, hoping that leading Sheena down this track might also prompt a change in topic. The awareness she had for Miles was definitely there but that didn't mean she had to do something about it, neither did she want to discuss it.

'Hush. I can say what I like and assign titles to

whomever I choose because I am the incubator and I have spoken.'

Janessa shrugged her shoulders as though she didn't have a leg to stand on with an answer like that. 'You are absolutely right. Anyway...' she collected Sheena's cup '...I have to go. I don't want to be late for the meeting.'

'You'll come by later and give me an update?'

'On most things, yes.'

'Good.' Sheena lay back and closed her eyes, getting ready to settle down for a nap. 'Nessa,' she said softly as Janessa headed to the door, 'don't push him away. He's not Bradley.' The words were spoken quietly and with complete seriousness.

'Understood,' Janessa replied, realising she hadn't fooled Sheena one bit with her attempt at changing the subject. Her friend knew her far too well. 'Thanks, Sheenie.'

Sheena yawned. 'That's what friends are for.'

As Janessa returned to her office and gathered the papers she would need for the meeting—the first of many on the conjoined twins—she pondered Sheena's words. Was she resisting the attraction she felt for Miles simply because of the way Bradley had pulverised her heart? Was she too afraid to even take a tiny step outside her very comfortable comfort zone in case she once more ended up in tiny pieces?

Was she that much of a coward that she would deny herself happiness simply because she'd been burnt so badly in her past?

Possibly.

CHAPTER SIX

THREE days later, after several meetings with key personnel as well as the hospital administrator, Miles arranged another one-on-one meeting with Janessa in her office. He had initially suggested that they meet in his apartment to discuss the upcoming operations the twins would require over a soothing cup of herbal tea, but even the thought of being alone with him, in his apartment, made her entire body quiver with nervous apprehension. Her office was definitely safer.

Ever since the kiss, Janessa had been overcome by masses of tingles every time she'd seen him. She'd constantly thought about him on the other side of her apartment wall, her curiosity about him increasing, and although she wanted to keep him at arm's length, she also wanted to know as much about him as possible.

Every look he gave her seemed to linger just a fraction of a second longer than normal. If he accidentally touched her hand or brushed past her during the normal course of any day in the NICU, she wasn't able to hide her quick intake of breath as her body suffused with heat.

'As you know, in order to separate the girls, they'll need extra skin to cover the actual incision site. Therefore, one of the first procedures we'll be performing once they're stable and healthy is to insert tissue expanders beneath the skin in order to grow extra skin in that area.' Miles lounged in the chair, relaxed and completely comfortable in her presence. Janessa had to admit that whilst he had the ability to set her body on fire with just one look, she, too, liked spending time with him in this way.

Under the guise of work, even though it was necessary work, for her to know exactly what procedures and steps would be taken with regard to separating the twins, she liked that she was able to spend time with him…like this…alone. He never talked down to her, always explained things thoroughly and answered any and all questions she had. Sometimes she thought she asked too many questions but he never became impatient, insisting that he would rather answer her questions a hundred times over so she knew what to expect than risk making mistakes.

He was thoughtful, too, and always the gentleman. Tonight he'd arrived in her office with a bag full of take-away Chinese food. 'Thought we might get hungry,' he'd stated as a means of explanation when she'd raised her eyebrows at the gesture. And so there they sat, papers and documents spread out before them on her desk, the scent of Chinese food filling the air as they ate and discussed the various aspects of the different surgical procedures.

'I have to confess, I have very limited experience when it comes to tissue expanders. It's just something I haven't come across that often. I have, however, read every paper you've written on this subject and the techniques you've used during the surgical procedures,' Janessa remarked quite enthusiastically, and was rewarded one of Miles's heart-melting smiles. Tingles flooded her body as she smiled shyly back at him. She still felt strange admitting she was such a big fan of his work.

Apart from that very first day in her NICU, when he'd been jet-lagged and completely exhausted, he'd been relaxed and friendly, as well as being totally in control of the specialised neonate team they were pulling together to care for the girls post-delivery. No one in either the NICU or Maternity had a bad word to say against him and half the women would swoon every time he came near. Janessa, however, hoped she wasn't as obvious whenever she was near him.

'Have you ever seen the operation performed?' He

used the chopsticks with ease as he lifted another mouthful of food to his lips.

Janessa sipped her green tea. 'Many years ago, in a two-year-old. Never in a baby. I think it's fascinating how the body can grow extra skin through this means.'

Miles nodded, impressed with the way she seemed eager to know everything about the twins' upcoming surgeries. 'It's much the same as how the skin expands in a pregnant woman.'

'Where do we order these special little bags?' She looked at the picture on the information she'd been studying then back at Miles. 'They're made of silicone, right?'

'That's right. They have a tube attached to them. In some of the older children we might leave the edge of the tube showing outside, making it easier to fill, but for the twins it's easier if the filling tube is just under the skin, thereby decreasing the risk of infection.'

'Which is the last thing we want.' She finished her noodles and used a napkin to wipe her face, before sipping the last of her green tea. Miles watched, delighted that she was the type of woman who didn't worry about her figure but instead seemed to have a very healthy appetite. Even when they'd been at the Italian restaurant, Janessa had eaten each course with appreciation instead of nibbling on a salad. It wasn't that she needed to watch her weight, far from it. She was perfectly proportioned…very perfectly.

He forced his thoughts back to the present, to the operation details they were discussing. 'Exactly. The bags will be gradually inflated over a number of weeks.'

'How long will the whole procedure take? I mean from the time the tissue expanders are inserted until there's enough new tissue for them to be removed?' She started to pack away her rubbish, tidying up, making things ordered and neat again.

'Approximately two months. We want to grow this new tissue slowly and carefully. Then, after another small operation, the expanders are removed and *voilà*—new tissue.' He, too, finished his food, and she held out her hand to take the empty container so she could dispose of it. 'Thanks.' He smiled as he wiped his face with a napkin.

Janessa smiled widely. 'That's what I love about medicine. The new breakthroughs in technology that make so much difference to the lives of our patients.'

Miles couldn't help but smile at her words, at the excitement she seemed to exude in discussing these surgeries. 'You really do love your job, don't you,' he stated.

Janessa met his gaze, feeling a little self-conscious. 'Of course. Don't you?'

'Most days.' He paused and sipped his green tea thoughtfully, watching her closely. 'Tell me, Janessa, have you ever thought of expanding your horizons?' At her blank look, he continued. 'You're excited by surgery. Have you ever thought of doing more training?'

Janessa was stunned by this idea. 'Uh…no. I'm more than happy where I am.'

'Don't get me wrong,' he added quickly. 'I think the work you do here is brilliant. You're well respected, you're highly skilled and Adelaide Mercy is lucky to have someone like you in charge of their NICU, but there's still more you could learn.' He leaned in a little closer, closing the distance between them, wanting to get his point cross. 'I could teach you.' His tone had dropped a level and the look in his eyes was more intimate than professional.

She was sure he could teach her, and not just about surgery! The way this man made her feel was something she'd never felt before. With Bradley, the love she had thought would last a lifetime had run its course in a matter of years, and even though he'd initially made her feel all special and nice, it was nothing compared to the far more adult feelings she was constantly experiencing with Miles. Just one smouldering, sexy look from his deep blue eyes and she was almost hyperventilating with repressed excitement.

She eased back in her chair, needing to put a bit more space between them. Breathing out slowly, determined to get herself back under some sort of control, Janessa nodded slowly. 'Thank you for such a generous offer, Miles but…um…I'm fine here. Doing my job, working alongside my friends and, at present, caring for Sheena.'

Miles held her gaze for another split second and then eased away, watching her carefully. 'Family is very important to you.' It was a statement, not a question.

'Very.' She paused and then found herself saying, 'Especially when you're left all alone.'

'Do you mean Sheena? I don't mean to pry but where is the father of her twins?'

She hadn't been referring to Sheena but she was more than relieved he hadn't realised she'd been talking about herself. 'Jonas? He's long gone.' Janessa rolled her eyes in disgust.

'So he's alive?'

'Oh, yes. Alive and well and living with his new wife in Brazil or Mexico or some other sunny place where he can be selfish and demanding and ruin other people's lives.' Her eyes were dark, filled with intense dislike. Miles hadn't thought it possible for her beautiful features to be marred with such emotions but it was quite clear in both her expression and the way she talked of the unknown Jonas that she didn't like him one little bit.

'But he knows she's pregnant? He knows about the babies?'

'Yes—yes, he does.' Janessa sighed heavily, not really wanting to blurt out Sheena's past to Miles but also knowing that anything she said to her friend's doctor regarding the babies father would remain confidential.

'Jonas high-tailed it out of Adelaide the instant Sheena told him she was pregnant or, more to the point, when Sheena was determined to see the pregnancy through.'

Miles raised his eyebrows, both perplexed and puzzled by this information. 'He didn't want to have children?'

'Correct. It was part of the reason why they married in the first place. Sheena had been told years ago that she would never have children. Jonas didn't want children, either. When Sheena discovered she'd actually been able to conceive, she was so happy, so ecstatic. It was like a miracle.'

'She thought Jonas would feel the same way.' Miles nodded.

'He didn't. Instead he took it as grounds to file for divorce. He told her that if she didn't abort the pregnancy, then as far as he was concerned their marriage was over because he wasn't throwing away any of his money or time or any part of *his* life on a bratty little kid. He left when six weeks later we discovered she was having twins. Another eight weeks down the line we discovered the twins were conjoined.'

'You say "we". Don't you mean *she*?'

Janessa smiled. 'No. I mean *we*. As you've already come to realise, Sheena is well loved, respected and protected by the staff in this hospital. What she's going through is huge and none of us are going to let her go through it alone. That's what family is all about, hence the *we*.'

'You don't plan on having a family of your own one day?'

Janessa was momentarily stunned by his question and the image of Connor flashed before her eyes. Her Connor. Her baby boy. The child that never was. 'I…don't know.'

'Surely you've thought about it? Marriage? Children? Quiet weekends? School runs? Real family time?'

'Once, perhaps, but not any more.'

'Once? Bad experience?'

'You could say that.'

'You were…married?' he fished. He knew it was wrong to delve into her past but the more time he spent with her, the more curious he became. Why wasn't a woman as incredible as Janessa involved with someone?

'Briefly.' She sighed and stood, turning her back to him. 'It didn't work out.'

'Do you know why?'

She laughed with a hint of irony. 'We were young. Too young. But we were so sure that we were really in love, that we were mature enough to understand the commitment we were making to each other, and when our parents realised we weren't going to be talked out of it, we tied the knot.'

There was sadness in her eyes and a despondent tone in her voice.

'How young?'

'Eighteen.'

'Both of you?'

'Yes. I guess we thought it was the real thing but we were wrong.' She shook her head and sighed. 'When things became too intense, too scary, too grown-up, I think we both knew we'd been kidding ourselves. We separated when we were twenty and were divorced by the time we turned twenty-one.'

'Hard lessons to learn. You've never thought about marrying again?'

She held his gaze. 'No. After that it was far easier to remain married to my career.'

'Which has obviously worked out well for you?'

'Yes.'

'Focusing on work can take your mind off a lot of things. Work is always there to see you through, no matter what disasters life throws at you.'

'You sound as though you're talking from experience.' It was her turn to fish.

'I was married.' He spoke the words quietly, surprised to find that he wanted her to know about his past. The fact that he was becoming more and more interested in this woman with each passing hour he spent in her company, it seemed only right to tell her about Wendy.

'Didn't take?' Janessa was secretly thrilled he was sharing this with her. Miles had such a knack for not making her feel as though she was the only one walking out onto a unsteady ledge all alone.

'Quite the opposite.'

'Oh.' She was surprised by that statement. Was he hiding a wife somewhere? She'd always just assumed he wasn't married. Sheena hadn't said anything about him being married but, then, Sheena hadn't stayed in contact with Miles during the past ten years since they'd worked together. Was Miles still married? It only confirmed how little she knew of him but before she could question him, he continued.

'My wife, Wendy, and I worked together for years, just colleagues, just friends, and then things slowly started to change into something more. We'd been married for almost two years when she died.' Miles stared off into the distance, remembering his past.

Janessa wasn't quite sure what to say for a moment but she knew what she wanted to do. She wanted to go to him, to put her arms around him, to say she was sorry for the loss he had suffered and the heartbreak he must have felt. She stayed where she was, keeping her physical distance from him whilst emotionally she felt more connected to him than before. 'You were lucky,' she stated.

'Yes.' He nodded and slowly exhaled any tension he may have felt in sharing his past with Janessa. 'Yes, I was.'

A more comfortable silence seemed to envelop them both, Janessa sighing as the tension and anxiety from her past slipped away. 'My parents were lucky.' She spoke the words softly, looking off into nothingness as she remembered. 'Their marriage was real and strong and I guess Bradley and I thought we'd be the same. I thought that my marriage would be as happy and as honest and as open as that of my own parents.'

'Where is Bradley now?'

Janessa shrugged. 'In Tasmania. We exchanged Christmas cards for about ten years but then it drifted off. We're both very different people now from who we were back then.'

'It was an amicable divorce?'

Janessa thought about the pain and heartbreak they'd both suffered when their son had died. Poor Connor. So little. Too premature to survive, and medical science hadn't been as great back then as it was today. It was because of her son and the amazing team of specialists that had treated him that she'd entered this speciality, as though to honour his memory and to help mothers who were praying for their babies' lives. Both she and Bradley had been stunned at Connor's death and things had never been the same between them after that. She'd put her hope and trust in their marriage, that together, as husband and wife, they would find a way through their pain, but he simply hadn't been able to cope.

'I guess you could say that,' she finally answered. 'I certainly don't hold any malice towards him. He wasn't to blame for what happened to us and neither was I.'

He sensed there was probably far more to it than

she was admitting. No divorce, however amicable, was ever easy. Besides, he'd pried enough for one night and finding out more about her didn't help the way she made him feel. He still had to work alongside her, the sweet, summery scent she wore winding itself around him, drawing him in, enticing him to know more.

Living next door to her in the residential wing, knowing she was so close yet so far, sitting reading a book, overcoming the plumbing problems as she showered, sleeping peacefully in her bed…was also starting to become something of a problem and he'd started to wonder whether perhaps he should look around for a place to rent, outside the hospital grounds but close enough that he was readily available.

He would continue to tell himself that Janessa Austen was just another colleague, in another hospital, in another city that he would soon be leaving. The fact that she was the first woman who had piqued his interest since Wendy was a miracle within itself. She'd built a family for herself here and it appeared she had no intention of leaving. He needed to move, needed to be challenged with his work because that way he didn't have to consider what might happen should he choose to, once more, spend his life alongside someone permanent…and

Janessa was just the sort of woman who would fit that job description.

He'd tried the happy family road before and it had ended in loneliness. Moving around, shifting every three to six months to a different location, a different country, going where the work took him, was the life he'd chosen and one he wasn't giving up simply because he was attracted to the intelligent and incredibly beautiful woman sitting opposite him.

'I'm sorry if you felt I was prying into your past. I most certainly didn't mean any offence by it,' Miles remarked after a moment, attempting to bring their thoughts back to the here and now.

'You were curious about me.'

He shrugged, feigning nonchalance. 'It's not uncommon for me to be curious about those I work with.'

'But I'm guessing you rarely follow through on that curiosity. You'd rather keep yourself to yourself, do your job and then leave. Which piques my own curiosity. Why? Why do you move around so much, Miles? What is it that you're running away from?'

'Who says I'm running away from anything?'

It was her turn to shrug. The man had just told her his wife had died and perhaps that had been enough to keep him on the move. 'I guess it appears that way when facts show that for the past six or seven years, you've never stayed in any one place longer than twelve months.'

'How do you know that?'

'Oh, come on, Miles. You're the man that everyone wants when it comes to conjoined twins. I can look you up on the internet and find a dozen or so different photographs of you and your team celebrating another successful spate of operations to separate conjoined twins, and most of them are at different hospitals around the world.'

'Maybe I just go where the work is.'

'Yes, but why? I'm guessing you're not bored with the work you're doing so if you're not running away, are you looking for greener pastures? A place where you fit? Where you feel comfortable? At home?'

'Why do you want to know?' he asked after a moment. She was getting close. She was asking him questions that he hadn't been asked by anyone in a very long time. He'd suggested that she expand her horizons, that she learn more, perhaps even travel with him so he could teach her more about the complicated and challenging world of conjoined twins. It shouldn't be such a stretch that as a homebody she would be curious as to why he didn't seem able to settle in one place. He couldn't blame her. He'd pried into her life and asked questions, so it was only fair.

'I'm…intrigued by you,' she remarked honestly,

holding his gaze for a long moment. The atmosphere between them began to intensify and after a second she breathed out slowly and walked towards the door. She opened it and leaned against it, looking out into her unit. Some babies were crying, others were sleeping and some were being fed. They didn't understand time—they didn't care if it was the middle of the night or the busiest part of the day. They all had needs, special needs, and she and her staff were on hand to provide them.

'We're a pair, Miles. Both determined to stay in control of our lives. Both wanting to focus on our careers and not risk even the slightest bit of compromise…and yet, whenever we're in a room like this, together, intimate, quiet, the tension is so tight it would take more than the sharpest scalpel to slice through it.'

Janessa looked over at him, tipping her head back against the door, revealing her smooth long neck, her hands behind her back giving her a relaxed and open posture. Her guard was down and the look in her big, mesmerising eyes was one of complete honesty. 'Do you think there's any real hope for people like us, Miles?' Her tone was free and soft and tired. 'People who are always trying to control the world around them?'

Miles swallowed, his heart beating wildly as he

drank his fill of the vision she made. He wanted to go to her, wanted to close the remaining distance between them, wanted to take her into his arms and to press his mouth firmly to hers. Didn't she have any idea just how alluring she was right now?

He shook his head, more to steady the burning need inside him to go to her than to answer her question.

She sighed again and looked away. 'I didn't think so.'

Another four days passed with, both of them confused by the emotions they felt for the other hiding behind their professional personae. The special clothes that had been ordered for the twins arrived and both Janessa and Sheena had a wonderful time looking at the gorgeous little outfits. There had been meetings every day, Miles going over the finer points of what to expect once the twins were delivered.

'The actual C-section is straightforward, but once the twins are out we'll need to be focused on stabilising them as soon as possible,' he'd said to Kaycee, Ray and Janessa who, along with Miles, would make up the initial postnatal care team. As far as planning for Ellie and Sarah's arrival, things seemed to be well on track.

Tonight, though, Janessa sat in her office and

looked at the mound of paperwork before her. She had planned to spend most of today out at the air-field, up in her glorious Tiger Moth biplane, whisk-ing away the cobwebs and setting her world to rights. Instead, she'd been in the unit for almost twenty-four hours straight, desperately concerned about a little baby, Philip, who had made his appearance in this world far too early at twenty-three weeks. Now, two weeks later and after a couple of doses of indomethocin to close the hole in his heart, it ap-peared surgical intervention may be necessary.

'Twenty-five weeks is not good,' she'd murmured to Kaycee as she monitored Philip's oxygen intake. 'Plus he's developed necrosis of the bowel.'

Still, the NICU staff would monitor him closely in the hope that the struggling baby would continue to fight for his life. For now, though, they'd man-aged to stabilise him as best they could but Janessa knew that if tiny, tiny Philip was going to survive, he would have a long and hard fight ahead of him. If he did require surgery, though, Miles, as the most experienced neonate surgeon they had, would per-form it and Janessa was relieved to have him here at such a time.

While they were in the hospital things seemed to be under control, but in the evening, when she returned to her apartment in the residential wing,

Janessa needed to call on all of her self-control *not* to think about him. Whether it be in her dreams or trying to guess what he was doing on the other side of the paper-thin walls that separated them.

She'd even taken to putting on headphones and listening to soothing music in order to help shut out images of Miles, next door...preparing food in the little kitchenette, sitting reading on the second-hand furniture, fighting with the taps to get the plumbing to work properly, lying in his bed at night...half-naked...hands behind his head, his muscles flexing, the blankets only partially covering his firm torso...

'Nessa?'

'Hmm? What?' She looked up from the work at her desk and met Ray's worried gaze. She shoved aside the ridiculous fantasies of Miles and focused her thoughts. 'Philip?'

Ray nodded. 'He's not improving. His oxygen requirement is thirty-five per cent and slowly increasing.'

Janessa sighed with sad resignation. 'I'll call Miles. It looks as though he'll have to operate on Philip after all.'

'Someone say my name?' Miles asked as he headed towards Janessa's open office door. His eyes met hers and for a fraction of a second they gazed at each other, veiled acknowledgement of the repressed awareness still coursing between them, before shifting their focus away and back to more important matters.

'It's Philip.' Janessa's face twisted as though little Philip's pain was her own, and in some ways it was. Philip's mother, Violet, was a seventeen-year-old girl who hadn't even known she was pregnant until two weeks ago. The fact that Janessa had been a young teenage mother herself meant she could empathise with poor Violet.

Miles nodded, already aware of the seriousness of Philip's case, and slowly exhaled, feeling the weight of the situation.

'Let's go and review him again,' Janessa replied. Philip was too young, too premature, too sick, and yet she wanted to do whatever they could in order to give him the best chance at fighting. They headed over to where Kaycee was closely monitoring Philip.

'We have to try,' she implored, looking directly into Miles's blue eyes, almost pleading with him to make things better. 'We have to try.' This time her voice broke on the words. Miles nodded and placed a hand on her shoulder. The touch wasn't romantic or sensual. While the warmth from his hand seeped into her body, she understood the show of support and solidarity his touch evoked.

'You're right, even if that means surgical intervention.' Thoughts of being unable to help his own little baby, the eight-month-old dying in his mother's arms during the horrific train crash, came back to haunt him. Miles knew he would do everything he could in order to give Philip the best chance possible. 'We owe Philip that much.'

With his words and his touch, Janessa felt a certain level of relief from her exhausted and frazzled nerves. Miles understood. Miles was also concerned about Philip and he knew they had to try.

Swallowing over the dryness of her throat, she breathed in a cleansing, calming breath and nodded. 'Thank you, Miles.' There was another beat where the two of them just stood, just stared, just absorbed, before he quickly dropped his hand and turned away.

'I'll go and speak to the mother.'

'Violet,' Janessa said.

'Pardon?'

'The mother. Her name is Violet and… Do you mind if I come, too?'

'No. Not at all.' Miles was pleased she wanted to join him as it only proved once again just how much Janessa cared about her patients, not only the babies but the mothers as well. Miles turned to Ray. 'You're trained in neonate theatre procedures, aren't you, Ray?'

'Most certainly, sir,' Ray replied, rolling his 'r's.

'I'll go and prepare the theatre and contact the anaesthetist.'

'Excellent.' Miles returned his attention to Janessa and swept his arm across his body. 'Shall we, Dr Austen?'

Janessa nodded and together they headed to Maternity where the young mother was lying in a bed, staring unseeingly out the window. Janessa drew the curtain around the bed, giving them some privacy from the other mothers in the ward.

'Hi, Violet.' Janessa smiled at her. 'How are you feeling? Any pain?'

'I'm fine.' She tossed the words out carelessly as though she didn't care about herself but sat up in the bed, gripping the sheets with both hands. 'Philip? What's happened? Is he all right? Has something gone wrong?' Her words tumbled out too quickly and Janessa instantly went over and put her hand reassuringly on the young mother's white knuckles.

She hated giving people bad news but she'd learned over the years that the best way was the direct way, combined with heart-felt compassion.

'Philip isn't doing too well at the moment. The hole in his heart is causing him more problems than his little body can deal with,' she began.

'We need your permission, should surgical intervention be necessary,' Miles continued, and went on to explain to Violet why Philip might need this surgical procedure. Throughout the entire discussion Miles was intrigued by Janessa, watching the way she seemed to relate on a personal level to Violet. There was vehemence in her words and repressed pain in her eyes. It wasn't only that she was being considerate to her patient, there was something deeper in her words, in the way she was making sure that Violet understood everything, in not talking down to the teenage mother. The compassion Janessa offered was complete to the point of perfect and it made him wonder whether something had happened to Janessa.

After they'd obtained Violet's permission, they headed back to the NICU, Miles still curious about his colleague. Janessa was quieter now, subdued but still direct in her actions and steadfast in her determination to do everything possible for Philip.

On entering the NICU, Miles headed off to the theatre and Janessa washed her hands thoroughly before heading over to Philip's humidicrib where Kaycee was still keeping vigil. She reached in and touched the little baby's stomach, stroking gently, crooning to him.

'We'll help you, sweetheart. As much as we can. We'll do everything possible. Be strong.'

'It doesn't look good,' Kaycee said a moment later.

'I know but even admitting that doesn't feel right.'

'He's too young. Even now, the risks are...' Kaycee trailed off, realising she didn't need to voice the thoughts both women were thinking. Janessa sighed, pain piercing her heart for the tiny life.

Soon it was time for Philip's surgery and after Ray had collected the baby from the NICU, Janessa went and scrubbed, pulling on her professionalism, ready to assist Miles. When he started performing the keyhole surgery on the tiny anaesthetised baby, Janessa found herself becoming more fascinated by his skill, and by the end of the surgical procedure, which had been undertaken with such precision and grace, she stood in compete awe of Miles and his abilities.

She'd read his articles and she'd always known he was the best. It was the reason why she'd requested he be the neonate surgeon in charge of Sheena's twins, but being here, watching him...it had only helped to solidify in her mind just how incredible Miles Trevellion really was. He was perfectly suited to this work, and although, through his publications, she'd been able to learn of his academic career and the way he'd become so specialised in this field, she had no idea what had prompted him to enter into neonatology in the first place. As a surgeon and col-league, he had her utmost respect but even as they degowned, she couldn't help but wonder what it was that made the man tick.

That, however, was an area she'd already marked as dangerous to enter. Hadn't she lain awake at night, wondering about him? Hadn't she tried to school her thoughts so she didn't dwell on the unanswered questions that didn't seem to want to leave her mind?

Deciding she needed a distraction and to get out of the NICU, and knowing she was leaving Philip with the best possible care, she headed up to the maternity ward to check on Sheena.

'He was amazing,' she said to her friend, her face alive with appreciation.

'I thought you weren't allowed to discuss patients with me,' Sheena remarked.

'I'm not discussing the patient, I'm discussing Miles and the way he performed the surgery.'

'Sounds as though you're really becoming…attached to the man.'

'Purely in a professional capacity,' Janessa quickly pointed out. 'It only proves that he is the most perfect doctor to be looking after your babies. It's right for him to be head of this team. Your girls…' Janessa reached out and put a hand on Sheena's abdomen, and one of the girls instantly kicked her, as though to say, *Hello, Aunty Nessa* '…are going to be just fine.'

'I know. With you and Miles looking after them, I *know* everything will be perfect.'

The two friends hugged and Janessa stayed for a few more minutes. 'I'd better get back to the unit.'

'Do you think Philip has a chance now?' Sheena asked as Janessa headed towards the door.

'A better chance than before but he's so…prem, Sheena. So small. So weak.'

'And how are you holding up throughout it all? Teenage mother? Very sick baby? This can't be easy for you, Nessa.'

'I'll be fine. What happened to me happened a long time ago.'

'Mm-hm.' Sheena didn't sound as though she believed her. 'Just know that if you need me, I'm here for you. I may be just a human incubator to my girls but for you I'm forever your friend.'

Janessa smiled. 'I know. You're the best, Sheenie. Anyway, I'd best get back to the NICU.'

'You will let me know what happens? Either way?' Sheena's words had been calm but firm. 'Lift the gag order for this one. Please?'

Janessa looked at her friend, seeing the concern, knowing Sheena had seen these same or similar circumstances before. They both had. They both knew the odds. Even with Miles's brilliant surgical skills, it might not be enough to tip the scales in Philip's favour.

'OK. Rest, though. I'll talk to you later.'

Janessa headed back to the unit and after getting an update on Philip, who was still heavily sedated, she headed to her office. She had a lot to do but didn't want to do any of it. She sat there for a good half an hour, trying to concentrate, trying to get her brain to focus on the mounds of paperwork before her but to no avail. At a knock at her door she immediately looked up, glad of the interruption.

Miles opened the door. 'Sorry to bother you.'

'It's fine.' She beckoned him in and indicated the seat opposite her desk, the one he'd sat in all sharp and direct on his very first day here. This time, though, he was more relaxed, more calm. He'd obviously showered and changed after surgery and his casual trousers and polo shirt seemed to fit him to perfection. Janessa worked hard to ignore the way he moved, ignored the way the man was the whole package—handsome, intelligent and caring. Everything she'd ever wanted in a man, sitting before her. She clenched her hands tightly beneath the desk, more as a way of releasing her own frustration at being so drawn to him than anything else.

'How is he?' She didn't need to say anything else. All of them were equally concerned about Philip.

Miles frowned. 'Not doing as well as I'd hoped.'

Janessa nodded. They both knew the outlook wasn't good but they were still determined to do everything they could to help him.

'I've just come from seeing Sheena.'

'I was up there earlier. Just needed a break.'

'Me, too. She told me you've lifted the gag order on this one. Do you think that's wise? The chances that Philip could die are extremely high. You don't think news like that will elevate Sheena's blood pressure?' There was the slight hint of censure in his tone and Janessa felt the sting.

'No. I don't. Not this time. This time it's different and we both know it. She knows Philip's prognosis isn't good. The gag order mainly pertains to the running of the hospital, especially anything from the paediatric unit. This… Philip…he's different. Sheena and I have always shared these deep exchanges with each other. It's what we do. It's how we support each other. It's why we're such good friends.'

'You've obviously been through a lot with each other. Anyone can see how strong the bond is between the two of you. It's nice. Deep, abiding friendships. They're rare.'

Janessa couldn't help but wonder if he was referring to his wife, the fact that he'd mentioned they'd

been good friends before the relationship had pro-
gressed. 'Yes, they are.'

'Do you think we might be able to have that?'

'A deep, abiding friendship?' she wanted to clarify.

'Or something like it.' There was an earnest tone
to his words.

'I've only known you for just over a week, Miles.'
She spread her arms wide. 'I've known Sheena for
almost twenty years.'

'We certainly have a good grounding for a friendship. We like each other. We respect each other. We
seem to share a similar sense of humour.'

Janessa pondered his words for a moment, deciding that if they simply agreed to remain friends for
the duration of Miles's stay, it might actually help
them to deal with the electrifying pull they felt towards each other.

'It's one thing to be colleagues and neighbours but
friends would be nice,' he added when she didn't
immediately answer.

'Friends.' The word was spoken slowly, as though
it was filled with deep reflection. Sighing, she stood
and walked towards the door, gazing out into the
unit for a long moment. Then something changed.
The hairs on the back of her neck started to prick
and she closed her eyes, listening closely, her back
straightening, her entire body tensed. Everything

else, trying to define her relationship with Miles, trying to control the way he made her feel whenever he was near…everything disappeared as she concentrated and listened to her intuition.

Miles noted the instant change in her demeanour, shifting briskly from open and sultry to one of instant apprehension. 'Something wrong?' he asked, standing up but not moving towards her. Distance. He needed to keep his distance.

'It's quiet.' Her tone was filled with concern.

'It's not that quiet. I can still hear a few babies making noises.'

'Not that sort of quiet.'

'Ah. You mean…something is about to happen?'

'Yes.' She looked at him and this time, all he saw was the look of a concerned neonatologist following through on an instinctive reaction.

'Philip,' they said in unison, and walked quickly over to where the little baby lay. He was sleeping, his breathing shallow and rapid.

If Philip was strong enough to survive, then young Violet would have her work cut out for her as babies born this early often ran the risk of neurological complications, such as autism or cerebral palsy. Her heart went out to both mother and child for whatever might happen within the next twenty-four hours.

'Something wrong?' Kaycee asked as she continued to monitor Philip.

'I don't know,' Janessa responded.

Kaycee picked up Philip's chart and handed it to Miles, who read it. 'I only did his obs two minutes ago. He's as stable as he can be, poor little lamb.'

Janessa accepted the chart from Miles and glanced at the information before looking at Philip once more. 'I don't know. There's just…something not right.'

'Instinct.' Miles nodded. 'The best weapon we doctors have and on the rare times that we don't trust it, heavy prices can be paid.'

Janessa could hear something, a tinge of sadness, a strong dose of regret coming through in what Miles was saying, and while she agreed with him one hundred per cent, she also noted that he was talking from personal experience. Had ignoring his instincts led to his wife's death? She pushed the thought aside, focusing on the wee baby struggling to fight for his life.

'Janessa has amazing instincts,' Kaycee confirmed.

'What do you think it is?' Miles asked.

'Seriously, I don't know. Something is…off. There's something not in line with normal parameters yet all his obs are fine.' She returned the chart to Kaycee and shook her head.

'So you're going to stand here and watch him?' Miles asked as Kaycee headed off to deal with another baby who'd just woken, his healthy little cries filling the nursery.

'Yes.'

'Fair enough.'

'What about you?' Janessa glanced across at him, both of them standing on opposite sides of their patient.

'You're right. Looking down at him now, there's something…niggling…something not quite…'

Before Miles had finished speaking, the machines monitoring Philip's heart rate started to beep noisily, Janessa noting that the tiny chest had stopped rising and falling. She quickly touched the baby, tickling his feet in order to stimulate a response. Sometimes babies needed to be reminded to breathe but this simple stimulation didn't appear to be working.

'No response,' she reported as Kaycee rushed over. Miles had already pulled on a pair of gloves and was hooking his stethoscope into his ears. Kaycee grabbed the Laderal bag and handed it to Miles so he could resuscitate Philip. Miles gently squeezed the bag to give the baby some breaths as Janessa pulled on a pair of gloves.

'He's still desaturating down to fifty per cent.'

'He's just not picking up.'

'We can do this. We can help him.' Miles's words were firm and controlled. He looked over at Janessa. 'Let's do our jobs.'

CHAPTER SEVEN

'OXYGEN at forty per cent.'

'No more apnoeas,' Janessa told Philip. 'Caffeine, Kaycee. Wake him up.'

'I'm on it.' Kaycee was already injecting the caffeine into Philip's drip in order to stimulate a response.

'His hypothalamus is too immature. It's not receiving the signals, not computing,' Ray murmured as he brought the intubation trolley over.

'Oxygen desaturating.'

'Increase oxygen to sixty per cent.'

'Are the umbilical lines clear? Still working?'

'Yes.'

'Prepare dexamethazone.'

'No response to caffeine stimulus.'

'Oxygen still desaturating.'

'Boost to one hundred per cent. Prepare adrenaline.'

'Chest X-rays?'

'Get the machine ready.'

'He's still not responding.'

'Bag him.'

They all worked together, each of them doing their utmost in order to save Philip's life. It wasn't looking good and they all fought harder.

'Body's changing colour. Going grey.'

'No. No. Let's get him ready to intubate.' Miles was still pushing. Janessa was working equally hard.

'Administer adrenaline. Come on, Philip. Hang in there.'

Janessa took over the bagging to give Kaycee a break, putting her finger over the hole of the Neopuff mask and lifting it again, getting the oxygen into Philip's brain. Her fears that it was already too late, that even if they were able to save him right now, it might be too late to stop severe trauma to the oxygen-starved brain. In the distance, as though it was far, far away, she could hear the noise of a young girl crying. Violet. Violet was there. She'd picked a terrible time to come and see her son…then again, maybe it was the right time after all.

'Colour still grey,' Ray murmured, and Janessa could hear the dismay in her colleague's voice.

'Ready to intubate,' Janessa said, and received a quick glance from Miles. He shook his head, the movement almost imperceptible, but she caught it. 'We have to try,' she urged him.

'Lips are turning blue,' Kaycee reported, her tone as despondent as Ray's.

'It's over, Janessa.' Miles's tone held complete sadness.

'No. We can do this. We can save him. We have the skill.' She reached for the laryngoscope but Miles put his hand over hers.

'It's over.' He took the instrument from her and met her gaze.

'No.' The word was torn from her, filled with anguish and sorrow. 'No. We have to—'

'Nessa.' The use of her nickname, hearing it come from Miles's lips, his deep voice laced with resignation, managed to break through her denial. 'It's over. Let him rest in peace.'

Janessa looked over at Philip, his lifeless little body just lying there, and her mouth went instantly dry. Flashes of Connor lying in almost exactly the same position… She blinked and swallowed. 'Call it,' she rasped.

'Time of death, ten past two.' Miles's voice was hollow as though it was an effort to force the words out.

'He was too premmie. Poor little love didn't have the strength to fight,' Kaycee murmured as she and Janessa stood looking down at the tiny, lifeless body. It wasn't easy. It was never easy to lose a patient but when they were so new to the world, so young and helpless, relying on the doctors to do their very best to save them…

The tears wouldn't stay where she wanted them and despite her most valiant efforts, they started to blur her vision. She swallowed over the lump in her throat and tried not to sniff. 'I'll go and tell Violet.'

'No.' Miles's tone was firm. 'I'll do it.' He met Janessa's gaze and she almost gasped at what she saw. The pain, the raw, grinding emotion seemed to flood from him directly into her. There was no hope in his eyes, no promise of any kind, just a well of deep, personal heartache.

She swallowed again, her dry throat not making it at all easy. As their eyes held, somewhere in the back of her mind she realised that he was waiting for her agreement to his statement. He would go and deliver the bad news.

'No young mother should have to face this.' With that, he turned and walked over to where Violet was with Helena, near the front desk of the NICU. Janessa watched, waiting for the moment when utter heartbreak would come over Violet's features. As Janessa stood there, watching, waiting… Miles's words penetrated her mind. 'No young mother should have to face this.'

What did he mean? Was he going to stop Violet

from seeing Philip? From achieving closure? No. She wouldn't allow it. All those years ago, after they'd told her they hadn't been able to save Connor, she hadn't been able to face seeing his lifeless little body lying there. Bradley had gone, had said goodbye, but she had been too distraught.

It hadn't been until that night, that first night without him near her, after Bradley had gone home, that Janessa had changed her mind. She'd needed to see him, to see for herself that he was really gone, to achieve the closure the staff had encouraged her to find. When she'd spoken to the nurse, they'd arranged for her to be taken to the mortuary, to a small viewing room with comfortable chairs and soothing pictures on the wall.

There, the medical examiner had brought out her little boy. He'd been wrapped in a white blanket with little blue aeroplanes on it. She'd sat. She'd held him. She'd kissed him goodbye.

She wasn't going let Miles stop Violet from seeing Philip. Violet needed closure. She needed to be able to say goodbye to her baby, otherwise she might well live the rest of her life carrying around the scars of grief and mortification.

'Janessa?' Kaycee's soft tone brought her thoughts back to the present. 'Do you want to go fill in the paperwork? I can get him ready for his mother to see—'

'We'll do it together.' Janessa nodded, and as a strained, uncomfortable silence fell over the NICU she and Kaycee worked quietly and efficiently to remove the attached equipment before wheeling Philip's crib into the empty emergency bay. This way, the young mother would be afforded the privacy she would need.

Janessa looked over to where Miles was still standing next to Violet, the young mother crying on Helena's shoulder. She wasn't going to allow anyone to stop Violet from having access to Philip. Drawing in a deep breath, squaring her shoulders and clearing her throat, Janessa wanted to let Violet know that Philip was ready for a final cuddle.

No sooner had she taken two steps towards them than Miles helped Violet to stand and started to escort her in Janessa's direction. Janessa stopped. He was bringing her over? At that moment, Miles looked up and saw her.

'Ready?' he asked softly.

'Ready?' Janessa was momentarily confused. When she'd presumed Miles hadn't wanted Violet to see Philip, it was obvious now that she'd grabbed the wrong end of the stick.

'For Violet to say goodbye?'

'Yes. Yes, of course. Right this way.' When Miles had said, 'No young mother should have to face this,' Janessa now realised he'd been referring to the entire situation of losing a child. It showed her once again how wonderful Miles really was. He was so kind and caring and… She shouldn't be thinking about him in such a way but right now she couldn't help it. Seeing him so considerate, so compassionate stirred something deep within her. He was quite a man.

Poor Violet was as white as a sheet as they led her to where Philip lay, peaceful and quiet in the crib. Janessa felt her eyes starting to sting with tears again and she pushed them away, quietly trying to clear the lump in her throat, pursing her lips tightly together in order to keep herself under control. Professional. She had to somehow remain professional.

'We're very sorry for your loss.' It wasn't a platitude that came out of her mouth but heartfelt words as the young girl looked at her lifeless son, wrapped in a small baby blanket.

'Can I hold…?'

'Of course.'

Miles ushered Violet to a chair and Janessa tenderly picked Philip up and handed him over. The girl looked at him for a moment, before rocking gently to and fro. She bent and kissed his little head and then started to sing a soft lullaby.

With the sweet, innocent sound filling the air around them, Janessa found she wasn't able to hold it in any longer. Tears ran silently down her cheeks, her heart filled with pain and anguish for what this brave young girl was going through. Without looking at Miles, she said softly, 'Take as long as you need, Violet. Excuse me.'

She managed to make it to her office and was able to shut the door before a gut-wrenching sob erupted from her body. She didn't seem able to stop the free-flowing tears and she blindly made her way to her desk in search of tissues. She dabbed at her eyes and quietly blew her nose but the tears and pain didn't stop. They would, eventually, she knew they would, but for now, if she didn't let this emotion out, she would burst.

She heard her office door open but didn't turn round, knowing it would be Kaycee come to join her for a quick cry. This wouldn't be the first time they'd shared their grief when losing a patient.

'Janessa?'

She gasped at the sound of Miles's deep voice, her vision still blurred as she glanced over at him. She couldn't believe he was seeing her like this, all red-eyed and sniffly, being highly unprofessional and giving in to her emotions because one of her patients had died. It wasn't the first time. It wouldn't be the last. But each one had affected her in the same way.

'Oh, Janessa.' His words were almost wrenched from him, and before she knew what he was about he'd closed the distance between them. 'Come here, honey,' he murmured, and gathered her into his arms.

She went willingly.

Janessa knew there wasn't anything romantic or suspicious in Miles's offer to hold her. She told herself that all he was doing was offering comfort, sharing a moment that had touched both of them. She swallowed over her dry, scratchy throat and leaned against him, unable to believe just how being held by him, feeling his warm, firm arms around her, was giving her back her strength and self-control.

Neither of them spoke. Neither of them moved. Her tears started to quieten and she hiccupped a few times. Throughout it all, Miles simply held her. It felt glorious and wonderful and she couldn't believe how much she'd missed having someone to just hold her.

The warmth of his body, the beat of his heart beneath his chest, the whole aliveness of him radiated through her and for the first time in a very long time she felt as though she might actually be able to cope with her past. Comfort. Relief. Hope.

'I was prepared,' she said after a moment, 'for her to hold him, to kiss him, to say goodbye.' She breathed in, still hiccupping a little and allowing his glorious scent to wash over her. 'But I wasn't prepared for her to sing to him.'

'A child singing to her child,' he murmured, his deep voice rumbling beneath her ear.

'She grew up. In that one instant I watched her go from being a scared teenager to a young woman who had already lost too much.'

'She has family,' he stated. 'They'll help her through it. It's what families do.'

'Yes. It's what families do,' Janessa agreed, knowing she needed to move from his arms, to break free of his hold because it would be far too easy to stay there, to keep drawing comfort from him... But the comfort was already starting to change to total awareness of being held against his firm, muscled chest.

She glanced up at him, swallowing when she saw the way he was looking down at her. His gaze dipped momentarily to her lips and she felt the sweet whisper of his desire wash over her. He still wanted her, was interested in her. Nothing seemed to have changed since the last time he'd been this close to her…the night he'd kissed her.

Sighing, the warmth from his gentle visual caress causing the butterflies in her stomach to take flight, she licked her lips, unsure how they had become so dry suddenly. He closed his eyes for a brief moment, clenching his jaw before once more looking at her. Did she have any idea of the allure that surrounded her? The way she was drawing him in, making him want to throw caution to the wind, to forget that they were colleagues, that they were supposed to be professionals, and kiss her—properly this time, instead of the accidental meeting of their mouths, which seemed to have been burned on his brain?

Forward. She was urging him forward, somehow pulling him from the past, his deep, darkened past where he'd ended up all alone, and was drawing him into the future. Forward. Giving in to the urge to kiss Janessa, to draw her closer into his arms, to devour her mouth with his own, was a definite step towards moving on with his life. So many of his close friends, people he worked with on many different conjoined twin surgeries, had been telling him for at least the last twelve months that it was time.

He hadn't known it himself until he'd met Janessa. Now here she stood. In his arms. Looking up at him while he was looking down at her, the mood between them becoming more and more electrified with each passing moment.

'Nessa.'

The instant he breathed her name, the instant it came to his lips and filled the silence around them she started to tremble. She also eased away, spinning from his arms, breaking the contact, needing the space as she rubbed her hands up and down her arms. Miles shoved his hands into his pockets, cleared his throat, and took a step back as Janessa moved behind her desk and pulled another tissue from the box. Even as she performed the action, he could see that her hands still weren't quite steady. It gave him hope. To know that it wasn't just him who was feeling this way but that she was as much affected by him as he was by her.

'Thank you, Miles… For the…er…comfort. It was…appreciated but just so you understand, I'm not in the habit of losing my control on a regular basis.'

'I understand completely. Special circumstances.' He swallowed, his Adam's apple sliding up and down his long neck. Janessa glanced at him then and noted that not only was there the hint of repressed desire but something else…there was something else hidden in his tone…something she'd seen earlier… What was it? It only took another moment of looking at him for her to remember the way he'd looked when he'd insisted on breaking the horrible news of the baby's death to Violet. There had been something there…something deep and moving and highly personal.

Janessa angled her head to the side a little. 'Wait a second.' Her words were soft and in no way accusatory. 'You were affected, too, weren't you?'

At her words, Miles closed his eyes for a brief moment before looking at her once more. 'More than you know.'

'It's never easy to lose a patient.'

'No. No, it's not.' Gone was the desire and out came the hurt. She'd never seen his eyes reflect such a hidden yet incredibly powerful emotion. Most people in the world made every effort to repress things or events that had happened to them in order to function with some semblance of normalcy. It appeared Miles was no different.

She paused, noting the hint of gut-wrenching pain in the way he spoke. He wasn't just speaking from a personal angle, he was speaking from his heart, and it was a heart that had been shredded. She recognised the anguish, she felt the pain he was exhibiting, she could read the symptoms because she'd felt them herself…felt them when her own son had died. Following through on an instinct, treading very carefully, she asked softly, 'Miles? When you lost your wife…was there…? I mean, did you have any… children?'

'Yes.' The one word was covered in heartache.

'Oh, Miles.' Janessa sighed, her heart turning over for him.

'One child. One baby boy. He was eight months old. We had eight glorious months with him. Although he was a bit sickly to begin with, in the NICU for the first two months, after that he was a strong, healthy, strapping baby boy…who died in his mother's arms.'

'It must have been devastating for you both.'

'No. Not for Wendy.'

Janessa frowned, unsure what he was trying to say. Miles looked at her, his blue eyes, which were so usually filled with joviality and direction, now bleak and cold. 'We were travelling by train in Europe,' he said. 'There was an accident, a bad one. A horrific train crash. We were all involved. Wendy was holding Patrick and when the train derailed…' He stopped for a moment. 'I was thrown around, multiple fractures, lost consciousness. When I woke I was in hospital. Wendy and Patrick were listed among the dead.'

'Miles.' Janessa's heart wrenched with sorrow for

him and she walked to his side, taking his hand in hers, linking their fingers together. 'I'm so, so sorry.'

'We were in the middle of nowhere. That stupid train crash robbed me of my family.' He shook his head. 'I was alone.'

Janessa squeezed his hand. 'I know how you feel. I do. I really do, and I'm not just saying that to make you feel better. I know what it's like to lose people you love...*babies* you love.'

Miles looked at her, recalling the way she'd been so vehement and determined to help Philip, the way she'd spoken to Violet as though she really did understand. 'You had a child, too?'

'I did. A boy. Connor.' As she spoke his name, she smiled. 'He was wonderful.'

'How old?'

She shrugged. 'Newborn. Twenty-five weeks' gestation. Just a touch older than Philip, but almost twenty years ago they didn't have half the equipment we have now. Today he might well have stood a fighting chance but, also like Philip, he was just too prem.'

'Is that why your marriage ended?'

'The loss of a child is never easy to cope with.' She shook her head. 'Bradley and I were just children ourselves, pretending to be grown-ups, but it was no good. I made impulsive and irrational decisions back then and it's taken me years not only to trust my own judgement but to trust others, not necessarily in the medical field but on a personal level. Any marriage break-up makes you really question yourself, makes you cautious of opening yourself up again. After Connor's death, we were both floundering in a sea of confusion, too young and too inexperienced in life to cope with the emotions we both felt, and in the end we realised the wisest thing we could do was to call an end to our marriage, to admit that we'd failed and move on. It was one of the hardest things I've ever done, to admit to that failure.'

Janessa dropped Miles's hand and moved away.

'Oh, Janessa.'

'So, you see, I *do* know how you feel. I know how Violet feels right now. Sitting out there, holding her baby, saying goodbye.'

'It still hurts.' His words were a statement, not a question.

She nodded in agreement. 'After all these years, it still hurts.'

Both of them were silent for a moment before Miles said softly, 'It appears we have more in common than we originally might have realised.'

'Perhaps that's what drew us together in the first place?'

'Janessa—' He stopped and raked a hand through

his hair before continuing. 'What do you say about becoming friends?'

'Get to know each other better?'

'Exactly.' He shifted and put his hands into his trouser pockets. 'We're going to be working closely together once the girls are born. Co-ordinating treatment, practical hands-on care, not to mention the preparation for the surgeries.'

'What are you suggesting?'

'That we spend time together because then that way we have some hope of finding common ground where this attraction isn't the first thing coming between us whenever we're together here at the hospital.'

Janessa thought for a moment. It would be good to be able to be in the same room as Miles and not be so aware of him. Perhaps he was right. Spending time together in a social capacity might actually benefit them rather than hindering their working relationship. 'You make a fair point. Well…I guess we could go flying.'

Miles blinked once. 'Flying?' He paused, remembering that she'd mentioned something about flying before.

'Sure. It will get us out of the hospital. We'll be out in the open, fresh air, blue skies, destressing and letting all our troubles float away on the wind.'

'Flying? You're serious?'

'One hundred per cent. I'm not talking about the big commercial jets that take you interstate or overseas. Just a nice small aircraft. Gliding around in the blue sky, enjoying the sensation of a complete carefree existence…if only for a short while.' Janessa sighed. Even thinking about it was helping her to relax, to calm down, to push the past back where it belonged. Miles, however, was still looking at her as though she came from a completely different planet. 'Or we could do something else. We don't have to go flying. You can think about it if you—'

'Sounds great,' he interrupted, still astonished to discover that Janessa liked flying. It wasn't the type of hobby or activity he'd have thought she would choose to do on her days off but, then, he was coming to realise that Janessa Austen was unlike any other woman he'd ever known. 'Flying.' He nodded once, accepting the decision, especially as Janessa seemed quite keen on the idea. 'In a small aircraft.'

'You're not claustrophobic, are you?' There was nothing worse than taking someone up in her Tiger Moth who had a fear of confined spaces.

'No. I'm fine.' He nodded again. 'So…flying. Good. Different, but good. When?'

'Good question. Um…' Janessa mentally went

through her schedule. They were now in the very early hours of Wednesday morning and given everything that had happened with little Philip, there would be quite a bit of red tape to get through. 'Thursday morning?'

Miles pondered that for a moment before agreeing. 'Nine o'clock. After ward round. I'll meet you here.'

With that, he turned and headed out of her office, gone before she could say anything else. Janessa stood there, not moving, and stared at her open door. She'd just invited Miles to come and spend time with her in a small and confined space! Was she completely insane? Even being here in her office was bad enough. The close confines of the Tiger Moth, the two of them, up in the air, able to talk to each other via the headsets…sharing an exhilarating experience…

But that was a good thing, wasn't it? His suggestion that they should get to know each other better, that they should stop trying to guess, stop trying to figure out what made the other one tick, was a good thing. The more time she spent with him, the sooner she'd discover some facet of his personality that would irritate her and therefore break the dynamic fascination that seemed to bind them together.

She would be taking him to her special place, the

airfield where she'd spent so much time, with her father as a child and later learning to fly. So many of her personal memories were bound up in that place.

With exhaustion weighing heavily on her shoulders, Janessa sank down into her office chair and closed her eyes, unable to believe her own stupidity. Had she really just opened herself up to share part of her life, a very important part of her life, with Miles Trevellion? Was she completely insane?

Apparently so.

CHAPTER EIGHT

AFTER writing up the paperwork for Philip and ensuring that Violet had finished saying goodbye to her baby, a weary Janessa escorted the young woman back to the maternity ward. Violet's obstetrician approved a sedative for her but Violet wanted Janessa to stay with her until she fell asleep.

Even sitting in the chair beside Violet's bed, Janessa's exhaustion level continued to increase. Once the young woman was asleep, Janessa headed to Sheena's room to check on her friend, surprised to find her awake.

She gave Sheena the sad news about Philip, and then checked Sheena's blood pressure, pleased that it was stable.

'It can't have been easy for you.' Sheena spoke softly, caressing her abdomen lovingly.

'It wasn't, but Miles…' Janessa yawned '…was a great help. He's so…' she sighed and closed her eyes for a moment '…comforting.'

'Really?'

Janessa didn't reply and Sheena chuckled. 'What?' Janessa asked a moment later.

'You are so exhausted, Nessa. Go to bed. Get some sleep.'

'I'm fine. I've been more tired than this before.'

'True but you weren't battling an attraction to your gorgeous colleague before.'

'You have a point.' Janessa's eyes were still closed as she sat in the chair.

'You're admitting that you like Miles?'

'Yep. Like him. A lot.' She yawned. 'Strange, isn't it? Never thought I'd be attracted like that to someone who won't hang around. Can't keep liking him, though. He's going to leave and I'll be all...' another yawn '...alone again.'

'You have me. You'll always have me, but I know what you mean.'

'I know.' Janessa opened her eyes and went to stand, wobbling a bit as she stood leaning on the chair until her balance returned. 'This always happens. When I finally stop, especially after a hectic day, my body just seems to go into complete shutdown.' She walked over and hugged her friend. 'You're the best non-legally-adopted sister I've ever had.'

Sheena laughed. 'Likewise. Now, go. Sleep.'

'I will, and just so you know, you're doing a fantastic job of being a human incubator. In fact, I'd say you're the best human incubator in the world. My mother was bedridden the entire time she was pregnant with me and I turned out fantastic.'

'Yes, you did.'

'Just think of how fantastic your girls are going to be.'

'I do. Now go and sleep before you fall down and hurt yourself.'

'Good advice. I feel so light-headed. 'Night, Sheenie.'

Janessa made her way out of Maternity and headed for the residential wing, very pleased that she was staying so close to the hospital. Sheena was such a wonderful friend and being raised an only child meant Janessa had often yearned for a sister. Now she had one. Although her parents had been able to have two babies before she'd arrived on the scene, both boys had been born with congenital heart defects. They'd both died within the first few months of their lives and back then the care for sick babies hadn't been as advanced as it was today. She'd often wondered whether Connor had a similar problem and perhaps that was why he'd died.

It was another reason why she'd chosen to specialise in the neonate field. To be there for women like Violet, to support close friends, like Sheena, to assist incredible surgeons, like Miles, and to read about the breakthroughs in research and technology.

Her mother had often told her how special she was, that she was their little miracle. A lump came instantly to Janessa's throat as she thought about her mother and in that split second, even though her mother had died almost eighteen years ago, her heart longed for just one more moment with her. To be held by her, to hear her mother's calm voice, to hear her sing a soft, soothing lullaby.

The image of Philip being held by Violet swam into her mind as she took the three flights of stairs up to her apartment. It was an image that came with its own sweet soundtrack and one that would no doubt remain with her for a very long time. Such loss, such heartbreak, such loneliness.

Janessa knew what it was like to be lonely. With no aunts, no uncles, no cousins, no siblings, no parents, it could have made for a very lonely life but all around her, here at the hospital, was a family she loved most dearly.

Then she had her friends out at the airfield, the friends who had known her father for most of their lives, who had watched her grow up, who had grieved with her when her father had lost his battle with cancer. Everyone around her combined together into one crazy big family and Janessa knew that she was truly blessed to be in such a place, but at the same time she would give anything to have one last hug with her mother or one last flight in her father's beloved Tiger Moth with him at the rear, flying them through the skies as though there really wasn't a care in the world.

Tomorrow, at nine o'clock, she would be meeting Miles to take him to the airfield to share her passion for flying. As soon as the thought entered her mind, she pushed it aside. It was almost four o'clock in the morning now and she was exhausted. It wasn't wise to think about the man when she was this tired because all of her defences were down. Add to that the memory of Philip's young mother singing to him and she felt emotionally drained. With her eyes blurring a little due to her sentimentality as well as the fact that she'd hardly slept in the past thirty hours, Janessa opened the stairwell door and exited onto the third floor, walking slap bang into someone.

'Oh, sorry,' she mumbled quickly, reaching out to rebalance herself and coming into contact with a wide, firm chest. At the same time, warm hands clamped around her waist and the weirdest sense of *déjà vu* settled over her. She breathed in, only to have Miles's spicy scent wind around her, drawing her in.

'This is starting to become a habit, Dr Austen.'

His deep masculine voice murmured near her ear. 'You. In my arms.'

'Sorry.' She glanced up, looking into his eyes, and instantly wished she hadn't. He was looking at her as though she were the most important woman in the world. His pupils were wide, his irises more blue than she'd ever seen before, and the care and need and desire she could see there made her body suffuse with anticipatory tingles.

'Don't apologise,' he added quietly. 'I'm not complaining.' His words were deep, rumbling through her, adding to the tingles by causing goose bumps to spread over her skin as his breath fanned her neck. His hands were at her waist, hot and warm and feeling as though they could burn right through her clothes. The sensations radiated throughout her, adding a flush of fire to the tingles and goose bumps.

When he touched her like this, looked at her like this, wreaked havoc with her senses like this, it was all Janessa could do to hold on to some semblance of rational thought. Working alongside him, being near him, watching his brilliance as he'd performed surgery on little Philip, had only served to enhance the delight and admiration she had for him.

Swallowing over the dryness of her throat, she worked hard to ignore the way her hands were pressed up against his chest, the firmness of his body beneath his shirt making her fingers itch to explore the area, to touch and caress every contour, to commit them to memory.

Even though she'd already been in his arms once that morning, this time was completely different from the platonic, friendly way he'd held her as she'd cried out her grief for the loss of the little life.

Ordinarily, he'd discovered Janessa to be strong and self-assured but now, as he looked down into the upturned face of this stunning woman, he could see tears glistening on her dark eyelashes. There was a vulnerability about her he'd witnessed when he'd walked into her office and seen her crying. A powerful, protective urge had overcome him then and now, standing here in the deserted residential corridor, was no different.

He wanted to protect this woman. From pain, from suffering, from being alone. He, of all people, knew how bad loneliness could be, and whilst he'd been surrounded by his parents and his sisters after the death of his wife and his child, it was the small hours of the morning—like now, when loneliness could be at its most powerful.

During his first week at Adelaide Mercy, Miles had been fighting the inexplicable, burning need he felt for Janessa Austen. Perhaps it was the fact that she'd taken him into her office on his very first morning there and told him off, showing him that she wasn't afraid to stand up for what she believed in. Perhaps it was the fact that she cared for not only her patients but for her staff as well, showing them unfailing loyalty. Perhaps it was the fact that she was like a petite dynamo who still looked far too young to be head of such a high-powered unit.

Or perhaps it was that she seemed to fit so perfectly into his arms.

He wasn't at all sure why he appeared to be so drawn to her. She was starting to open him up, starting to make him believe there could possibly be more to his life than simply working and travelling. Even now, as he held her, her body so close to his, her scent winding around him, enticing dormant senses back to life, he couldn't help awareness coursing through him. He swallowed and watched as her gaze flicked to his throat before settling on his lips for a brief moment then returning to his eyes.

His mind went blank as he realised she was looking into his own eyes, revealing emotions such as confusion, intrigue and veiled desire. It was the way she'd looked at him in the lift last week but this time the emotions were deeper, richer, more intense. He'd been out of the game so long, out of the need to seek female companionship, and now here was Janessa, causing him to want, causing him to experience, causing him to feel.

It was as though everything during the past week had lead to this one moment. It was the moment when Miles slowly began to realise that, for the first time since the death of his family, there were other possibilities in life than living it on the run from his past, hiding from his guilt.

Janessa swallowed and licked her lips, causing Miles to want to lower his head, to brush his mouth across hers, just for a second, just to see how she tasted. It wasn't the first time he'd wondered that and it wouldn't be the last. He was attracted to her. Powerfully and strongly. Now, though, right at this moment in time, they were both vulnerable. He could see it in her eyes. She was heavily exhausted and her defences were low.

This time, though, the tug, the invisible bonds that seemed to be binding them together were most definitely harder to resist. He really wanted to kiss her and that want was starting to grow into a need…a desirable need.

Although it felt as though they'd been standing there for an eternity, in reality it had just been a couple of minutes, but even during that short period of time he could feel Janessa's body starting to relax more heavily against his.

'Miles?' she murmured, her desire-filled eyes looking up at him. 'What's happening between us?'

'I don't know, honey, but I do know that now is not the right time to discuss it. You're exhausted and it's time for you to get some sleep.' With a valiant effort he tried to step back, to release his hold on her, but as he did, she stumbled and leaned against him again. 'Whoa, there.' He slid his arm more firmly about her waist. 'I think your exhaustion has most definitely caught up with you.'

Janessa yawned and nodded, feeling lethargic and sleepy and nice, being held so close next to Miles. 'Excellent diagnosis, Dr Trevellion.'

'Right, then. Let's get you settled. Where's your key?'

'My what?' She raised her eyebrows to look at him.

'The key to your apartment.'

Janessa frowned for a moment, then patted the pockets of her trousers. 'Not there. Darn. I must have left them in my office.'

'Oh.' Miles's quick mind filtered through his different options. He could leave Janessa in the corridor, run down stairs and get a spare key from the residential desk. He could put Janessa in his apartment and then go down… No! That one was instantly dismissed. Even the thought of having her sitting in a chair, waiting for him, no doubt sound asleep…the mental picture was too alluring.

Walking her closer to her door, feeling her lean into him as sleep started to claim her, he decided to try a different option, ridiculous as it seemed. He inserted his own key into her door. The lock clicked. He turned the handle. The door opened.

'Interesting,' he murmured.

'What is?' she asked, her words slightly slurred and as he looked down at her, realised her eyelids were already half-closed.

'Nothing. Come on, honey. Let's get you into bed.'

'Bed?' She roused as he walked her into her apartment. It took him a split second to realise the set up was the mirror image of his own apartment and he headed for the bedroom. 'I can't go to bed with you. I can't, Miles. I want to but we can't. You'll be gone in six months and my life will be here with painful memories and…' She yawned as he carefully guided her to the bed and pushed aside the covers.

'We're not going to bed together. Just you in your bed. Me in mine. It's safer that way.'

'Safer,' she repeated as she pulled the band from her hair, blonde locks spilling out against the red satin pillowcase. He pulled the covers over her, his gut tightening at the glorious picture she made. Eyes closed, body resting, face devoid of emotion. Unable to contain himself, he reached out and brushed her hair back from her face, allowing the pale strands to sift gloriously through his fingers. So silky, so soft.

Swallowing, he bent over her, pressing his lips to her forehead, knowing he shouldn't but powerless to resist. He breathed her in, closing his eyes as he committed the sensations to memory. The feel of her skin against his lips, the way her subtle scents surrounded him, the rhythm of her steady, even breathing.

'Sleep sweet, Nessa,' he whispered, before standing and striding firmly from her apartment, desperate now to push aside the longing and the loneliness that swamped him.

'Ready?'

Janessa turned and watched as Miles walked into her office, taking in the more casual attire of blue jeans, navy blue polo shirt and top-of-the-line running shoes on his feet. He looked so relaxed, so casual. Even the way he usually wore his hair was different, more ruffled and slightly spiked on top rather than brushed into a neat and ordered style.

On the first day she'd met him he'd been wrinkled and tired and ruffled and exhausted and even then he'd looked incredible. Today, though, his jaw seemed squarer, possibly due to the light stubble enhancing his good looks. It made him seem more relaxed, more rugged, more sexy.

She blinked once, twice and then forced herself to stop ogling him and to snap back into functioning mode. 'Uh…yeah…um, I mean yes. Sure.' She was standing at her desk, having just finished writing up some notes on her little patients. Five babies had been well enough to go home and seven had been moved to the maternity ward near their mothers. The unit was now back to a more reasonable level of occupancy and she knew her staff were more than capable of handling any emergencies that happened, although she seriously hoped for a quiet day.

'I'll get my things,' she murmured, and as she turned her back on him Miles couldn't help but take in her more casual attire. Up until now he'd only seen Janessa wearing tailored suits. Her skirts had all come to mid-calf and on the days when she'd worn trousers, she'd looked even more crisp and efficient.

He'd idly wondered if she wore the power suits in order to make herself look older and now, seeing her dressed casually in a pair of denim jeans and a knit top, her feet enclosed in brown leather boots, her hair still pulled back into a ponytail, he *knew* that was the reason for the stiff and starched suits because right at this moment she really did look about nineteen. All fresh faced and brimming with nervous energy.

Even when he'd tucked her into bed very early yesterday morning, he'd been mesmerised by her youthful appearance. Thirty-six? She looked anything but that old, and as she came towards him, a white scarf around her neck and a backpack slung casually over one shoulder, he was once again struck by how incredibly beautiful she was.

'OK. Let's go.' They exited her office, Janessa closing the door behind them, feeling the warmth of Miles's presence close to her.

'Can I take that for you?' he asked, holding his hand out towards the backpack.

She smiled politely. 'It's fine. It's not that heavy.' She felt so self-conscious, standing here in the unit, on her day off, feeling as though she was about to head out on a date with her new colleague. It wasn't a date. They both knew it wasn't. Didn't they? Her eyes widened imperceptibly as she wondered whether Miles thought that today was a date. It wasn't but she had no idea how to make that clear to him without running the risk of making a fool out of herself.

'Right. I guess we'll take my car.' She felt strange walking out of the unit with him, conscious of all eyes upon them. Why did it feel as though the two of them were getting ready to embark on something that would take their relationship from professional to personal?

At the door, she stopped and looked at Ray. 'You'll call me if—?'

'Yes, yes,' he muttered, shooing her away. 'Go. Fly. Relax. That goes for you, too, Miles. The two of you need a break, and with Sheena's due date creeping up on us, this might be the last free day either of you have in quite some time.'

'Good point.'

'Now, scoot. Some of us have got work to do.'

'Quite the instiller of confidence,' Miles remarked as they headed out of the hospital. The day was big and bright and the sky had barely a cloud. Perfect April day and perfect flying weather. As they walked to the rear of the residential wing, passing several staff car parks along the way, Miles couldn't contain his confusion. 'You did say we were taking your car, not walking to this airfield, right?'

'It's just in here,' Janessa remarked, a slight smile tugging at her lips. 'Charisma gave me permission to use one of the old ambulance sheds to store my car. Here we are.' She took a set of keys from her pocket and opened the side door to what looked like an old work shed. As they headed inside, she flicked on a light, illuminating the work benches, which were covered with various bits of machinery and all kinds of tools. The scent of oil and grease hung in the air as well as dust.

'Who does all of this belong to?' Miles asked.

'Hospital Maintenance. This is sort of a storage shed-cum-workshop for them. Through there…' she pointed to the closed door on their left '…is where the bigger machines, such as the lathe and the band-saw, are kept.' Janessa walked to another door, waiting for Miles to catch up as he looked around at the paraphernalia.

'Do you like this sort of thing?' she asked, her lips twitching at the way he was taking in the equipment. 'Are you a handyman as well as a surgeon?'

Miles smiled. 'I used to spend a lot of time in the shed with my dad when I was growing up. He was always inventing and making and building.' He nodded. 'They were good times.'

Janessa was surprised to hear him talk so openly of his father. 'That sounds nice. Memories like that are wonderful.'

'They are,' he agreed as he followed her through to another room.

'I used to help my dad out a lot, too. He was a mechanic,' she remarked as she flicked on the next light. With a flourish she'd practised a lot as a teenager, she whisked the protective cover off the car, then watched as Miles's eyes almost bugged out of his head at what he saw.

'That's a Jaguar E-Cabriolet.'

'I know.' Janessa set about opening the old wooden doors in order to get the car out. Miles, however, walked around the car, running his hand lovingly over the paintwork, peering inside at the wooden dashboard and making the same appreciative noises Janessa's father used to make. It made her smile.

'This is *your* car?' Miles slowly shook his head. 'You are a constant source of surprise, Janessa Austen.'

'Thank you…I think. You obviously appreciate cars.'

'I do. I race them.'

'What? And you call me a constant source of surprise. You said you liked to drive fast but race? As a doctor, I would have thought you'd understand the inherent dangers involved in car racing and—'

He held up a hand to silence her as the daylight flooded into the room. 'Controlled track race days. That's all. Nice and controlled. Emergency crews on standby just in case. I know the risks involved, Janessa, and I'm not so stupid as to ignore taking the necessary precautions. But this baby…' he stroked the car again '…is magnificent.' He looked up at her. 'Who did it belong to?'

'Why would you think it wouldn't belong to me?'

'Because it's a guy's car.'

'That's such a stereotype, Miles Trevellion.'

'I know. Sorry, but—'

'It belonged to my father. As I said, I used to help him.'

Again Miles stared at her with a new and enlightening appreciation. 'You really are a constant source of surprise.' He also hadn't missed the past tense in her words when she'd referred to her father.

She opened the car door and climbed behind the wheel. 'Do you mind switching off the light and closing the shed doors behind me?'

'Sure.' After that was done and when he was settled in the car, seat belt on, sunglasses covering his eyes, wind in his hair, Miles grinned and nodded. 'It purrs like the most contented of cats. Good to see you keep it in top-notch working order.' As he spoke, he again ran his hand over the leather seats. 'So nice.'

'Would you like to drive it?'

'Yes.' The answer was immediate. 'Will you let me?'

'So long as you realise that we're not on a race track.'

He gave her a look that said he wasn't that stupid.

'All right,' she relented. 'You can drive home.'

'Excellent.' Miles grinned and eased back into the leather, and as they drove through the city traffic, making their way south, he felt for the first time, in a very long time, mildly content. Was it the car? Was it the chance to get out of a hospital into the fresh air, to do something completely different? Or was it the woman beside him who was proving that he should never judge a book by its cover?

CHAPTER NINE

BY THE time they arrived at the airfield, almost an hour later, Janessa felt the weight of the past few days lift from her shoulders. When she'd checked on Sheena that morning, she'd discovered her friend had had a great night's sleep. She had listened to the twins' heartbeats and checked Sheena's vital signs, pleased with the results.

'Go. Have a day away from this place,' Sheena had encouraged. 'I promise to be good and do exactly as I'm told so that nothing goes wrong and you don't have to come back early.'

'Thanks. I'd appreciate it.'

'You and Miles deserve some time away from this place to figure out what on earth is going on between the two of you.'

'Wh…? Huh?' Janessa was robbed of speech and stared at Sheena.

'I lie here, in this bed, all day, all night. People come. People go. People talk—not about hospital cases,' she added quickly just in case Janessa thought that someone had broken the gag order.

'I see you. I see Miles. I see you and Miles. Both of you are dancing and it's the same dance. Both of you are moving in time with each other to the same beat. That's a good thing, Nessa. Good for him and good for you.'

'But he's going to leave,' Janessa blurted out.

'Maybe. You don't know that for sure.'

'Of course I do. Look at his life. Ever since his wife and son died, he's been an emotional nomad.'

Sheena's eyebrows hit her hairline. 'He had a son? Uh…he told me he'd been married when he first arrived here but he didn't say anything about a son.'

Janessa instantly paled. 'Oh. I thought you knew. I mean… The two of you were friends. You knew each other.'

'I worked with Miles ten years ago and he was as personable back then as he is now, although I do have to say that now that I think about it he's definitely more subdued but, then, most people seem to settle a bit more with age,' she'd pondered. 'But the fact that you know that about him, the fact that he's obviously felt he can confide in you, is huge, Ness.' She paused. 'Have you told him about…?'

'Bradley and Connor?' Janessa nodded and Sheena sighed a deep sigh.

'Well, well, well. In that case, the two of you *really* need to get away from this hospital. Head out to the airfield, whisk away the cobwebs of the past and look forward to the future.'

'*What* future? I don't know what this thing is that exists between Miles and myself and neither does he.'

'Then it's time to find out. Go. Go, go.' Sheena shooed her away, but as she headed out the door of her friend's room Sheena called, 'Oh, and take some photos for me. Perhaps just looking at them will help keep my blood pressure under control.'

Now, at the airfield, the warm, fresh air filling her lungs, Janessa climbed from the driver's side of the car and retrieved her backpack from just behind the seat.

'This is an airfield?' He lifted his glasses from his eyes and gazed out at the flat, wide open space, which had a backdrop of yellowy-brown hills and clear blue sky. There were large sheet-metal-clad hangars and about twenty cars in the car park. An old fire engine stood ready to do its job and about ten small aircraft peppered the immediate landscape.

'Doesn't it look like one? I thought the planes would have been a dead give-away,' she teased, feeling more like herself than she'd felt in a long time. She loved this place, so very much.

'I…well, yes, you have a point.' Miles smiled at her, intrigued with this new Janessa he was seeing.

From the instant they'd entered that old shed, revealing her incredible car, she'd been one surprise after the other. He was thoroughly enjoying it. 'It's just not what I expected.'

Janessa called a greeting to a young man of about eighteen years old who was walking by, a pair of large headphones in his hand. He waved back and Miles followed Janessa into what appeared to be a small café.

'Hello, Nessa,' a woman with silvery-blonde hair said from behind a large wooden counter, coming around to envelop her in a warm motherly hug. 'How are all your babies? And Sheena? Should be soon, shouldn't it?'

'Sheena is doing well,' Janessa replied, not even wanting to think about the past few work days and the way they'd all fought so valiantly to save little Philip. She stepped away from the embrace and indicated Miles, who was standing just behind her. 'Myrna, this is my new colleague, Miles Trevellion.'

'Hi. It's nice to—' Miles had been about to say more when he found himself enveloped in a warm maternal hug, which took him completely by surprise.

'Welcome. Welcome. Any friend of our Nessa's is very welcome here.' Myrna looked at Janessa and winked, saying in a stage whisper, 'Ooh, he's a right looker, this one.'

Janessa looked at Miles then back at Myrna, and couldn't help the blush that tinged her cheeks. 'Um... yes.' She walked round to the other side of the counter and picked up some papers, reading them. She did it in an effort to hide the way Myrna had embarrassed her, needing just a few moments to pull herself back together.

Miles leaned onto the top of the wooden counter and she could feel him watching her closely. 'Do you work here?' he asked. 'Is this what you do on your days off? Come and work here?'

'Work here?' Myrna laughed. 'Good heavens, no. Janessa's one of the shareholders who keeps this place open and functioning.' Myrna returned to the other side of the counter. 'Davie's been over *Ruby* and she's all ready to go, love. I know how eager you are to get on up.'

'Thanks, Myrna.' Janessa went to the shelf and pulled out a hardcover book, opening it up and beginning to write. Miles watched her, intrigued by this new facet of her personality. He saw the writing on the front of the book, which said 'Flight-plan/ Logbook—Janessa R Austen'.

When she was finished, she left the book with Myrna, Miles still watching closely. She met his gaze. 'I'll be back in a moment.' But before she moved she tipped her head on the side and looked at his broad shoulders, his firm torso and then nodded. 'Yes. I think it'll fit,' she rasped, her voice sounding a little husky, or was that just his imagination? The impromptu visual caress only increased his awareness of the undercurrents of emotions coursing between the two of them.

'What? What will fit?' he asked, but she'd disappeared into a back room. 'What's she talking about?' he asked Myrna, feeling a little dazed and confused. Janessa had invited him here for a bit of a joyride but he was yet to be introduced to his pilot. Janessa was obviously going up with someone called Davie. Perhaps he would be going up with Ruby? It was all very cryptic at the moment.

Myrna smiled at him. 'Ever been flying before?'

'Of course. I flew from the US to Australia last week.'

'Not like that, ya daft one.'

Miles raised his eyebrows. Daft? The last time he'd been called daft he'd been a teenager. Janessa returned before he could question Myrna further. She held out a leather bomber jacket to him. It was old, a bit frayed around the edges here and there, but it held a lot of character. 'Here. Put this on.'

'On? Why?'

She looked at him as though he was indeed daft. 'So you don't get cold. I doubt Sheena or anyone at the hospital will thank me if you return to work with a cold because you weren't adequately prepared for your flight,' she remarked as she pulled on a similar jacket, which she took from her backpack. She repositioned the white scarf around her neck then inclined her head towards the door, repressed excitement in her eyes. 'Come and meet Ruby,' she said with a cheeky grin, before walking out of the sliding glass door, across the wooden veranda and out the small gate that led to the planes.

'Ruby?' Miles followed Janessa and was astonished to see her walking over to a yellow Tiger Moth biplane with the words 'Ruby' painted in cursive on the side. '*This* is Ruby?'

'Who else would it be?' Janessa stroked the plane lovingly, much in the same way he'd stroked her car.

'In love with the old plane? Again, you are so full of surprises.'

She smiled. 'In love with my dad's old plane.' The look on her face was wistful with a hint of sadness.

'You really miss him.' It was a statement, not a question.

'I do. It was just the two of us for so long and now that he's gone…' She let her sentence trail off. She stroked the name 'Ruby', which had been painted on with a loving hand many years previously. 'Ruby was my mother. This plane was my dad's saving grace after my mother died. He bought it, restored it, spent so much time talking to the plane, as though he was still having conversations with my mother.' Tears of happiness and regret came into her eyes as she smiled sadly. 'He loved this plane. We both did.'

Both parents gone. Bad marriage. Stillborn baby. All alone. Miles pieced together everything he'd learned about this amazing woman and his heart turned over with yet another wave of deeper caring. 'You really are all alone?'

Her answering smile was tight-lipped as she moved around the plane, stroking it, checking it, making sure everything was in working order. 'Not really. I have close friends both at the hospital and here.'

'But no blood relatives?'

'No.' The word was small but audible. 'But I have memories.' When she spoke, there was a slight wobble in her tone and Miles watched her closely for a bit longer.

'Like flying in his plane? Or driving his car?'

Her smile instantly brightened. 'Exactly. He loved classic things, my dad.' She headed to the front of Ruby and spun the propeller around a few times, checking. 'Well, Miles,' she said with a heavy sigh,

'I think we're about ready.' She walked to the side panel and opened it, handing him a leather flying helmet, large goggles and a pair of large aviator headphones, with microphone attached.

He held the items in his hands for a moment, watching as she pulled out one for herself. First, though, she took out the band from her hair, the blonde tresses falling loosely around her shoulders, framing her face, the wind blowing them slightly, making her look like something out of a hair commercial.

His gut tightened with need and longing. He clenched his jaw in an effort to control himself against the absolutely stunning woman before him. She looked so young, so beautiful, so…untouchable.

'Problem, Trevellion?'

'Huh?' He blinked as though he'd just been dazzled by the sun. Instead, he knew he'd been dazzled by Janessa.

'Put them on,' she said, indicating the helmet, goggles and headphones he still held in his hands. 'Come on. I'm itching to get going.'

He stared at her for another long moment, her words slowly registering. '*You're* the pilot?'

'I thought that was obvious. I do remember saying I wanted to take you flying.' She shook her head. 'Here. Let me show you how to get in.' She started to give him instructions and Miles knew he had to click his brain back into gear otherwise they wouldn't be doing any sort of flying today.

He followed her directions, making sure he only stepped where she'd indicated, and all too soon he was sitting in the front seat of *Ruby*, Janessa standing on the wing beside him. She knew how to fly? First the Jaguar and now the Tiger Moth? When he'd walked into Adelaide Mercy last week, he'd never, in his wildest dreams, thought he'd be going flying with his neonate colleague.

So much had happened in such a short time and as Janessa leaned over him, reaching for the five different straps that would secure his body and buckle him into the seat, keeping him safe, all Miles seemed to be conscious of was the way her hair floated around her face, the way her scent enveloped him and the way her hand brushed his arm.

He was highly conscious of this woman and being this close to her yet again was not helping him to understand such a feeling. After Wendy's death, he'd vowed to concentrate on work, to help save the lives of others, as he'd been unable to save his wife and baby.

Now here he was, interested in another woman, a woman who had experienced pain and loss herself. Janessa was a woman who seemed to understand him, who seemed able to gauge his moods, to know what to say and what not to say. Ever since the other day, when they'd discovered just how much they had in common, their discussions about the conjoined twins had taken on a new level of power. It was as though now they understood each other's pasts, their drive to ensure everything went smoothly for the twins increasing.

'Miles?' Janessa's sweet voice penetrated his thoughts. There she was…beautiful Janessa with her flowing blonde locks and her sunshiny scent, the woman who was pulling him from the past into the present.

'Sorry,' he murmured, and shook his head. 'I missed that last bit.'

Janessa eased back, tilting her head to the side as she regarded him more closely. 'Is something wrong? You don't have to come up if you don't want to. I don't want to pressure you. I didn't tell you what we'd be doing in case you decided not to come at all.' And, she realised now, she'd *really* wanted him to come. Bringing him here, sharing this part of her life with him seemed the right thing to do…the next step in becoming friends.

'I'm fine with the flying. I just…zoned out for a moment. I'm fine, really. I'm already starting to relax.' He forced a smile and gave her his full attention.

He was enjoying all the wonderful new things he was learning about Janessa—the way she was not only extremely good looking but also incredibly intelligent; she also knew how to fly a Tiger Moth—that showed him how closed off his world had become. Since the death of his wife and child, Miles had brought in the boundaries his world, only letting in touches of light when it was needed most, just enough to keep him from tipping over into complete darkness.

Now, when he looked at Janessa, when he realised how smart and funny she was, it was as though she'd walked into his life and yanked open the curtains. Heavy, powerful sunlight seemed to flood into his life…opening the locked door to his heart.

'OK. What I need you to do is to put your hands either here on the side of the plane or up here above the instruments, but other than that, don't touch anything.'

'You'll be doing all of the flying behind me?'

'Yes. These planes are very finicky.' She secured the seat belt then pointed to the leather hat, goggles and headphones she'd handed him earlier. She plugged in the end of the headphone set so they could communicate. 'Put them on. The microphone will be close to your mouth. It's a little difficult to hear due to the wind but we'll get there.'

Being so close to him, giving him instructions and securing the harness had meant she'd come into close contact with him yet again and this time she hadn't tried to analyse the sensations such an action caused. She'd breathed in his scent, allowing it to wash over her, invigorating her entire body. Her mouth had been quite close to his own as she'd angled herself to make sure the straps weren't twisted. Her fingers had brushed the soft leather of the jacket he wore as she'd secured the belt at his waist.

She needed to right her thoughts, to brush away the effects of this man, or else she might not be able to fly the plane properly. Whilst she'd flown many of her friends in *Ruby* over the years, this was the first time she would be flying someone she was attracted to. Wanting to impress him suddenly seemed important. She knew it was crazy but that's the way it was.

Before she stepped off the wing, she turned her face into the wind, letting it blow her hair back and out of the way before she put the leather flying helmet on, quickly adjusting her goggles and aviator headphones. With her white scarf and leather jacket, she looked every inch the sexy pilot.

'How long have you been doing this?' he murmured, his voice deep, as though he was as affected by her as she was by him.

'Wearing sexy headgear?' she asked with a little smile.

He grinned. 'No. Flying.'

'Since before I could drive a car. Relax, Miles. You'll be fine. Just remember, don't touch anything. No levers, no gauges, no dials and leave those pedals on the floor alone.'

'Touch nothing. Got it, boss.'

'Hmm…boss, eh? I like the sound of that!'

With that, she jumped down off the wing, climbed into the seat behind him and waited for one of her friends to come and turn the propeller at the front of the plane to start it. Soon they were taxiing down the dirt runway, Janessa's clear voice requesting permission to take off.

'Ready, Miles?' When her voice came through his headphones, it was filled with wonderment, excitement and adrenaline. He didn't blame her. It was highly contagious.

'Ready,' he returned, and the biplane taxied down the runway before heading up, up and away.

Thirty minutes later, after flying over the sea, rolling hills and farmland surrounding the airfield, Janessa brought the aircraft in to land. When the wheels had safely touched down, Miles couldn't resist clapping and even gave a whoop of delight, which she heard through her headphones.

'Enjoy that?' she asked.

'Amazing! That was incredible. The wind on my face, the sun all around me, feeling as though I was one with this awesome machine… Yeah, Janessa, I enjoyed it.'

Janessa's own smile was bright and she was pleased she'd been able to share her love of flying with Miles.

She brought *Ruby* to a stop right next to the café. 'Door-to-door service,' he joked.

'We aim to please,' she said, before pulling out the connection on her headphones and pushing the microphone out of the way. She did a quick post-flight check before flicking open the buckle that had held her harness securely throughout the flight, the straps falling away. Climbing out, her goggles and headgear still in place, she bent over Miles to undo his large metal buckle but found he'd already done it. She turned to look at him and only then realised just how close they were.

'Thanks,' he murmured as he flicked the microphone in front of his mouth out of the way. Janessa swallowed, unable to move. She was standing on the reinforced part of the wing, hanging on to the rim of the plane, leaning over into the front passenger seat, her mouth literally millimetres from his.

'You're welcome.' Her heart was hammering wildly against her ribs and, given her present location, she was actually having a hard time breathing. Was it due to the way she was contorting her body or the fact that if she edged the tiniest bit closer, her mouth would touch his? She swallowed, knowing it was the latter.

He was looking at her lips, she could see quite clearly through her flying goggles that he was looking at her lips. The tension surrounding them crackled to life once more. They were colleagues; they would be working closely together for the next six months while he was here in Adelaide and then Miles would depart. Vamoose. Leave. She'd followed his career long enough to know he rarely stayed in one place. He was a man who shifted states and countries and continents, following the emergency calls of neonatology. She couldn't fault him for that.

She licked her lips, feeling self-conscious, and was about to move when she heard him groan.

'Don't.' The word was barely audible.

'Don't what?'

'Do that.'

'Do what?' she asked again, her gaze flicking from his eyes to his mouth and back again.

'You know exactly what you're doing.'

'I do?'

'You're drawing me in.'

Janessa swallowed again, her mouth and throat dry with anticipation, her heart pounding out such a quick tempo she thought she might become light-headed. 'Drawing you in?'

Her breath mixed with his, combining together along with the warmth of the day. Up in the air, with the breeze surrounding them, it had been exhilarating. Now, back down to earth, being so close to him, having him speak to her as though she were the most precious woman in the world, Janessa found him equally as exhilarating.

The spark was there, hot and powerful and refusing to be ignored. It was always the same when they were this close, when they were alone, when everything else in life seemed to disappear into oblivion.

Why did she have to be so close, so gorgeous, so… appealing? There was far more to Janessa than first met the eye and Miles couldn't help but acknowledge just how important she was becoming to him.

He should ease back, look away, make a move, something—*anything*—to break the bubble surrounding the two of them. How was it possible that within such a short time she'd been able to break through the walls, the barriers he'd spent years putting in place?

After Wendy's death he'd vowed to become one of those doctors who was more interested in his work than anything else. He wanted to help, to heal and to harness the potential of the people around him before high-tailing it. Allowing himself to settle down in one place wasn't on the cards. He wasn't meant for a life of domesticity. That point had been proven years ago when he and Wendy had tried to settle down.

And then he'd secured a job in Vienna. Head of Vascular Surgery. It had been too good to pass up but Wendy hadn't liked to fly so they'd taken the train.

His life had changed. The world he'd known had disappeared and from that moment on he'd made sure that he'd lived his life on the fringe. He'd completed more training, become a neonatologist, assisted with breakthrough surgery, written articles and papers, given lectures and presentations. He'd worked hard to get to where he was and now he liked his life and most definitely wasn't in any hurry to change it, or he hadn't been…until he'd met Janessa Austen.

From the beginning she'd been an enigma, appearing too young, too strait-laced, too appealing.

He'd vowed to keep his distance from her, to have his walls and barriers firmly in place, just as he always did, and yet here he was, in her Tiger Moth, having enjoyed every moment he'd spent with her from the instant they'd left the hospital.

How had she battered down his walls? How had she managed to get under his skin so quickly, so effortlessly? What was it about her that made him completely unable to resist her allure? He shouldn't be looking at her. He shouldn't be reacting to the way her pink lips parted to allow her tongue to wet them. He shouldn't be almost desperate to taste her…but he was.

He'd wanted to kiss her so badly yesterday morning when she'd been so exhausted that she'd all but stumbled into his arms. He'd wanted to kiss her after holding her close in his arms, comforting her after Philip's death, unable to believe they'd both been parents of children who hadn't survived. He'd wanted to kiss her as she'd stared at him across the conference table, and if he was honest with himself, he'd admit that he'd wanted to kiss her the moment she'd bawled him out in her office not one hour after they'd met.

He'd been drawn to her from the start and although he knew he'd be leaving in six months, although he knew the feelings he had for her couldn't really lead anywhere except to pain, he also knew he simply couldn't fight her allure any longer.

'Don't look at me like that, honey.' And before she could ask what he meant, before she could utter a word, her mind filled with excitement and confusion and trepidation, Miles had closed the minute distance between them and captured her mouth with his own.

Their flying goggles clanked together and at the sound Janessa went to pull back, realising this was wrong, that it wasn't meant to be happening, that she and Miles were colleagues...perhaps even friends... but not this.

Kissing was wrong.

Miles, however, was having none of it and merely angled his head a bit more so their goggles didn't clank as he pressed his lips to hers more firmly. Her body came to life at the touch, at the pressure, at the need that seemed to burst forth from somewhere deep within her.

She had no idea where such intensity had come from. She had no idea what it might mean. All she knew was that Miles had given in, had stopped fighting the internal struggle she'd previously witnessed in his hungry blue eyes, and for that she was incredibly glad.

Glad. She was glad he'd kissed her and as his

lips continued to hold hers captive, she was struck with the realisation that she hadn't been glad—truly glad—about anything for quite a long time.

'Janessa.' He edged back ever so slightly, her name a whispered caress from his lips.

'Mmm?' Her eyes were closed, her mind was spinning, her body felt as light as a feather. The way he made her feel was as though she'd breathed in helium and was floating up towards the sky, content just to be. The only other time she'd ever felt that sensation had been when she was up flying *Ruby*, forgetting the cares of the world… And now Miles made her feel that way with his addictive kisses.

Slowly, she opened her eyes and breathed in, his spicy, earthy scent tantalising her senses even more. He still had his goggles on, his headphones and his leather flying helmet—as did she. The sounds of the airfield, other small planes preparing to taxi down the runway, the smell of aviation fuel in the air as another plane refuelled, the wind blowing a gentle breeze around them…the world at large started to return into focus and she blinked as though to clear her mind.

'Uh…' She straightened up too quickly, almost knocking her head on the upper wing, and as she swerved to miss it, she overbalanced. 'Whoa!'

With a thud she fell to the ground, landing in a tangle.

'Janessa!' Miles quickly removed his headgear and goggles before carefully levering himself out of the seat and standing on the reinforced part of the lower wing. 'Are you all right?' But even as he asked the question, his gaze taking in the unruly sight of Janessa sprawled on the ground, trying to untangle herself from the headphone cord, which had wound itself about her leg, he felt his lips start to twitch into a smile.

She looked up at him and glared. 'Don't you dare laugh at me, Miles Trevellion.'

'Why not?' He stepped to the ground and without even offering her a hand up—which she would have most definitely refused—he bent and slipped his hands beneath her arms and lifted her to her feet in one easy move, the headphone cord untangling immediately.

'Let me go. I'm fine. I don't need any help.' She shifted away from him, completely embarrassed and annoyed for letting him kiss her, letting him touch her, letting him get under her skin. She pulled off her headphones and goggles before unbuckling the leather strap on the helmet and removing it, shaking out her blonde hair. Without another word, she stomped off through the gate and into the café without waiting for him.

He watched her go, sauntering along slowly behind her, knowing it was best to give her some room… give them *both* some room.

Why *had* he kissed her? Why had he given in to the urge and actually kissed her? Was it because their lives had run along similar paths? Was it because she knew exactly how he felt, surviving the death of a child? Was that a bond only people who had been in that situation could share?

It was definitely true, but he also could admit to himself that he'd been attracted to her, impressed by her, long before he'd discovered that piece of information. Knowing what drove them, understanding why they'd chosen to specialise in the field of neonatology, had opened the doors he'd kept locked for far too long.

Spending too much personal time with Janessa might actually become hazardous to his health, especially if she continued to be this constant source of surprise. She drove an incredible car, she flew not only a plane but a Tiger Moth and she tasted like strawberries. He liked strawberries.

As he headed inside, she was nowhere to be found, but Myrna was behind the desk. She held out her hands, accepting the headgear he still carried.

'What have you done to our Nessa, eh? She was all hot and flustered when she came in just now. That's not how she usually returns when she's been up for a relaxing flight in ol' *Ruby* so what have you done to her?'

Miles looked at the older woman, the woman who appeared to be in mother-hen mode, protecting her young. There was a determined look in Myrna's eyes that told him she wasn't in any mood for teasing. His own mother had worn the same look from time to time and he knew when to toe the line. It appeared honesty was the name of the game.

'Uh… I…' He cleared his throat, feeling like a recalcitrant teenager, especially as he shuffled his feet. 'Uh…I kissed her.' He didn't know why he'd confessed it, especially as when all was said and done it was no one's business but his and Janessa's. What he hadn't expected was Myrna's eyebrows to shoot up in surprise and a smile to spread across her face in utter glee.

'Really?' she asked with incredulity.

'Uh…yeah.' Before he could say another word, Myrna had come round the counter and embraced him in a large bear hug, even tighter than the one she'd given him when he'd arrived.

'Oh, I'm so happy. That's wonderful news,' Myrna babbled as she let him go, but slipped her arm through his, leading him gently to look at some of the photographs up on the wall. 'Come and take a look at some of these photographs. She was such a cute little poppet.' Myrna pointed at one of the photographs.

It was a black and white photograph of a man standing next to an old Tiger Moth, one arm resting on the plane, the other around a girl of about six or seven who was missing her two front teeth, grinning widely, her blonde hair flying in the breeze. Neither of them looked as though they had a care in the world.

'That's Janessa?'

'You guessed it. Her mother took that photograph. That was the day her father bought his first plane. Came out here a lot, they did. Then, of course, when his wife died, he sold that first plane and bought a different one.' Myrna showed him a different photograph. 'That's the glorious *Ruby*. Named the plane after his late wife. Never got over her death and it was over a decade later before he went to join her. Ahh… I tell you, Miles, that wee girl was born to be in the air.' She pointed to a different photograph in colour, one of Janessa taken only a few years ago, standing with the same man, although this time he looked sick and frail. Both of them were smiling but it was more for appearances than with the carefree spirit of years before.

'Over a decade later,' he murmured absent-mindedly as Myrna continued to talk. He shook his head. The poor woman. To lose her mother, her baby, her husband and then her father, too. For someone to come through such pain, such intense suffering gave him an indication of just how strong Janessa really was.

'A strong sense of family,' Myrna continued. 'That's what our Nessa has here, and we're all fiercely protective of her. And...' Myrna glared up at him '...none of us want to see her get hurt.'

Miles nodded. 'Understood.'

Myrna slowly shook her head. 'Did you *really* kiss her?'

Miles's smile was automatic. 'Yes, ma'am. I didn't mean to. Just sort of...happened.'

Myrna leaned in closer and patted his arm. 'That's the best way,' she whispered as Janessa walked back into the room.

'Ready to go, Miles?' she asked, brisk and efficient and more like the doctor he'd met on his first day at the hospital. There didn't appear to be any sign of the woman whose mouth had responded so ardently to his. He'd kissed Janessa! A colleague! He still wasn't sure why he hadn't been able to keep his distance, still wasn't sure what was going to happen next, still wasn't sure how Janessa felt about it.

Myrna turned to face Janessa. 'Leaving so soon, Nessa?'

Janessa smiled sadly at her friend. 'Sorry, Myrna, but duty calls.' She looked at Miles, her expression returning to one of complete seriousness. 'I've just received a call from the hospital.'

'Problem?' Miles was instantly alert, turning away from gazing at the photograph of Janessa as a little girl, so cute and adorable.

'Possibly.'

'Who called you? Ray? Kaycee? Is it one of the babies?'

Janessa shook her head. 'Sheena called me. She's worried.'

'Sheena's worried?' The look on Miles's face indicated how serious this might actually be.

'Yes, and you know Sheena. She's not the worry-wart type.'

'Get going, then, Nessa.' Myrna handed Janessa the car keys, which she had put on the counter when she'd arrived. 'Go and do what you need to do. Don't worry about *Ruby*. Davie will take care of her. You go and look after Sheena and those babies—and give her our love.'

Janessa nodded and hugged her friend close. 'I

will. Thanks, Myrna.' She gathered up her back-pack, jacket and scarf and headed for the door.

'It was lovely to meet you, Miles,' Myrna re-marked, giving him a sly little wink that wasn't at all sly, as Janessa witnessed the exchange. 'Come back again some time. Soon!'

'I intend to.' Miles held the door for Janessa and as they headed to the Jaguar he was surprised when she handed him the keys. 'Are you sure you want me to drive?'

'Safest and fastest way back, please.' She slid into the passenger seat and put on her seat belt. Her fingers rubbed at her temples, trying to calm the headache that had appeared the moment she'd heard Sheena's worried voice down the phone line.

Miles slid behind the wheel, adjusting the seat before turning to face her. 'Are you all right, Janessa?'

'No. No, I'm not.'

'Worried about Sheena?'

'Yes.'

'Has she called Riley?'

'She wasn't going to so I did. He's on his way to review her. He'll call me the instant he knows what's going on, given that it'll take us some time to get back to the hospital.' She shook her head. 'I shouldn't have come down here today. I should have stayed close. Sheena isn't given to over-statement and fuss. In fact, she abhors it so for her to call and tell me she's worried means there's definitely something wrong. Something bad.' Her voice cracked on the last two words, fear and panic, mixed with self-anger, lacing her tone.

Miles reached over and took her hand firmly in his. 'We'll get to her. Riley will call us. It'll be fine. Sheena and the girls will be fine.'

'But it isn't time. If the girls can stay put for at least one more week, things will be better,' Janessa protested irrationally, drawing an immense amount of comfort from Miles's touch. She should be withdrawing from him, she should be keeping her distance, especially after the way she'd responded to his kiss.

Miles had kissed her...*really* kissed her! The first time had been just a press of his mouth against hers and both of them had been surprised at the level of intensity that that brief moment had brought forth. Now, after his mouth had devoured her own, she couldn't believe how much she wanted a repeat. Being so close to him, having his mouth on hers, seeing that burning look in his eyes, caused her heart to pound out a powerful rhythm of want she'd been denying for...well, for ever.

She met his gaze. Even the thought of leaning

over and kissing him once more had the ability to bring a blush to her cheeks. How was she supposed to reject his offered comfort, his support, when now was the time when she really needed it? For so long she'd had no one except Sheena to comfort her when things went wrong, and now, right when she needed him, Miles was there for her.

She closed her eyes for a moment, finding it was all too puzzling, too confusing, and she'd be better off focusing her energies on Sheena rather than on trying to decipher the incomprehensible way Miles made her feel. He gave her hand one last little squeeze before letting go and turning the key in the ignition, the Jaguar's engine purring to life.

'Everything's going to be fine.' His tone was sure and firm and steadfast. 'We'll get to Sheena. We'll be there to help her, to give her what she needs. Everything will be fine,' he repeated. 'Believe me.'

Janessa opened her eyes and looked into his dynamic blue depths. She recognised the complete truth in his words. He wasn't just saying them to calm her down. He really *did* believe that Sheena and the girls would be fine, and Janessa believed him. She believed him! She was stunned to discover that she not only believed him but that she'd somehow become reliant on him.

The thought made her tremble and she quickly

slid her sunglasses in place as Miles drove out of the airfield car park. She believed in him. She relied on him. What was next? Would she wake up one morning and discover that she'd fallen in love with him? In love with the man who would one day leave her?

No. She couldn't do that. She had to remain strong, remain in control. She swallowed as he took her hand in his again and gave it another little reassuring squeeze, the sensation helping to calm her nerves but heightening the way she was drawn to him.

This wasn't good. If she continued to be affected by him in this way, she would be in real danger.

CHAPTER TEN

BY THE time they arrived back at the hospital, Janessa's mind had worked through almost every scenario there was. She'd had to stop herself from going to the worst-case scenario first because even *thinking* it had brought tears to her eyes.

Sheena was going to be fine. Sheena and the girls were going to be fine. Miles had said so but both of them knew that until they stood before their friend, until they could see face to face that she was indeed all right, everything was mere speculation.

Under Janessa's directions, Miles drove the car into the emergency bay at the front of the hospital, handing the keys to one of the orderlies who was more than happy to accept the job of parking Janessa's pride and joy back in the old shed.

As they rushed to the maternity ward, Miles could see the stress and strain on Janessa's beautiful face. His protective instincts kicked in and he found himself reaching out to hold her hand as they made their way through the long and busy hospital corridors.

He was silently pleased when she didn't reject his touch and, gripping her hand tightly with his own, they continued to walk fast, closing the distance between themselves and their friend.

When they arrived in the ward, the sister gave them a look of relief.

'There you are. She's been asking when you'd both arrive. Riley wants to get her to Radiology to do an ultrasound to check on the twins because according to the foetal heart monitors, nothing seems to be wrong and—'

'We know,' Miles remarked, keeping calm, even though he could feel nervous and anxious tension radiating from Janessa. 'Riley's already called us to let us know Sheena's status.' It was only as he stopped to speak to the sister that Janessa disengaged her hand from his and entered her friend's room. Miles didn't miss the sister's look of interest at the fact that they'd been holding hands. No doubt there would be fall-out, gossip, rumours circulating, given that they'd walked halfway through the hospital holding hands, and while he didn't care what people said about him, the last thing Janessa needed right now was to be the hot topic of discussion at every coffee break. For now, though, it was paramount that he get his head around what was happening with Sheena.

'Where's Sheena's chart?' he asked, holding out

his hand. There were already too many people in Sheena's private room and the sooner Miles read the observation charts and reports, the sooner he'd have a better idea of what might or might not be happening. Janessa had been very quiet on the drive back and he hadn't tried to get her to open up or talk. That was one thing he'd learnt over the years—women would talk when they wanted to but when they were quiet and contemplative it was best to leave them to their thoughts.

When Riley had telephoned information through, instead of relaying it to him Janessa had put her phone on loudspeaker and the two of them had been able to hear and talk to the obstetrician about what was happening. He'd appreciated that because it also showed him that where Sheena and the babies were concerned, Janessa really did trust him.

'Everything is within normal parameters.'

'That's what we can't figure out,' Sister replied.

'Riley's right. We need to ultrasound the babies. Sheena's blood pressure seems to be slightly raised but that could be simply anxiety. However, if we can't get Sheena's blood pressure under control, Adelaide Mercy's first set of conjoined twins will no doubt be born tonight. Pass me the phone. It's going to be far easier to have the ultrasound equipment brought to Sheena than the other way around. We need to keep her as stable and as settled as possible.'

Sister did as she was told and within ten minutes the sonographer entered the ward, accompanied by orderlies carefully wheeling the equipment into Sheena's room. Miles headed into the room after them to find Janessa standing by her friend, holding her hand, ready to offer whatever support was required.

'There you are, Miles.' Sheena smiled at him but even Miles could see how tired the mother was. 'Where have you been?'

'Doing my job,' he remarked as he came closer and kissed her cheek. 'Conferring with Riley and a lot of others.'

'Is that why he kept going in and out of the room?' Sheena sighed, leaning back against the pillows, showing her exhaustion. Miles knew right then and there, just looking at the mother, that it was time. Even as the sonographer squeezed lubricant onto Sheena's abdomen and started to give them pictures of the girls, Miles knew. He'd seen it too many times before.

He looked over at Janessa who, unlike everyone else in the room, wasn't looking at the screen but was looking at him. There was a question in her eyes, a question of concern, a question of vulnerability, a question of doubt. Miles's first instinct was to cross to her side, to take her into his arms and to tell her that everything was going to be all right, to reassure her, to give her the strength she'd need so that she could pass it on to Sheena.

He was only mildly surprised at such a need to protect her, to be there for her, given that it wasn't the first time he'd felt it. Too many times in the past week he'd wanted to do exactly the same thing, to protect and comfort her, and now that he knew how it really felt to have her lips pressed against his, how her mouth was the most perfect fit to his own, the sensations she evoked within him were definitely increasing.

She raised her eyebrows questioningly, as if to say, Is it time? Miles nodded, the action small but conveying so much. Janessa's beautiful brown eyes were filled with worry before she closed them, drawing in a deep breath and letting it out slowly. Then, when she opened her eyes, Miles recognised the professional neonatologist he'd worked with during the past week. She'd pushed her trepidation and anxiety aside, knowing she wouldn't be any good to either Sheena or the girls if she wasn't completely focused on what was about to happen. She'd told him on his first day here that she had the ability to do the job, and now he was seeing her words being put into action.

'Everything looks fine with the girls,' Riley commented, but looked at Miles for his reaction.

Miles, instead, looked at Sheena. 'You're exhausted. Your blood pressure hasn't improved in the past hour—in fact, it's increased.'

'The incubator has finished her job,' Sheena remarked, nodding as though she knew this was the way things would go.

'Almost,' Miles replied with a smile.

'You're the expert here, Miles,' Riley returned. 'What's your verdict?'

'Based on my experience, now that Sheena's blood pressure has started to rise, it means the girls are in danger and that things will start to break down. It's time. If we operate today, we'll get two healthy girls. If we leave it and monitor Sheena, we run the risk of the girls starting to fail. The thing with conjoined twins is that while you have to acknowledge that mentally they are two separate people, both with their own little personalities, the fact is that if one of them starts to fail, so will the other one. We want *two* healthy babies.'

Janessa nodded. 'Agreed.'

'Agreed,' Riley added. 'I'll head to Theatre and get

organised. Oh, and someone had better let Charisma and the PR people—'

'Already taken care of,' Miles remarked.

'Excellent.' Riley nodded and continued out of the room. The sonographer had packed up her equipment and the orderlies were wheeling it out again. The nursing staff had headed out too and within a matter of minutes it was only Janessa, Miles and Sheena left in the room, everyone busy doing what they needed to do in order for these babies to be born safely.

'Charisma. *Pffft.* PR. *Pffft,*' Sheena grumbled. 'Why can't I just be left to have my babies in peace? Why am I this big three-ringed circus?' Tears bubbled over and Janessa instantly comforted her friend.

'It's not fair, is it?' She wiped away Sheena's tears and looked at her. 'Everything's going to be fine.'

'Is it?' Anxiety, worry, confusion, pain and heartbreak were in Sheena's tone. She looked at Janessa and then at Miles, her lower lip wobbling. 'I'm scared,' she whispered, and Miles moved closer to place a hand on her shoulder, wanting to reassure her in every way he could.

'Janessa and I are going to be there every step of the way,' Miles confirmed. 'And just think, soon, very soon, you're going to be able to touch your baby girls. They're both doing well, Sheena. They're both as healthy as they can be and you've done the most incredible job of carrying them for so long.'

'Miles is right,' Janessa agreed. 'You've been the most incredible and powerful incubator. The best in the world.'

Sheena gave her a watery smile and then a little laugh. 'Thank you.' She looked at Miles. 'Thank you both.' She sighed heavily and then rubbed her abdomen. 'It's time, girls. It's time for the three of us to meet. Oh, what fun we're going to have.'

Janessa leaned forward and spoke in a stage whisper. 'And Aunty Janessa promises to buy you both lots of noisy toys to drive your mother crazy.'

Miles laughed and looked at the woman he'd kissed only a few hours ago. She was funny and smart and caring. Strong and brave and sensual… And she was becoming far too important to him.

Sheena's C-section was performed without complications. Riley, the obstetrician, was not bothered by the cameras in the room, which would record the event for posterity. Miles had always told her that the delivery was the easy part but the reason they'd had meetings to discuss the postnatal care so intricately was so they were completely ready the moment the babies were out.

'My fifteen minutes of fame and you can't even

see my best angle,' Sheena had joked as Janessa and Miles, Kaycee and Ray had stood by, waiting for the moment the twins were handed over to them. The instant the girls were carefully placed into their loving care, the neonate team focused on their special little patients. Ray and Kaycee worked closely alongside Miles and Janessa, inserting umbilical lines, steadying the girls' oxygen as they worked on them beneath large heat lamps over the specially designed crib.

'The first twenty-four hours are critical,' Miles had said at the different briefings they'd had during the past week. 'Even more so than with other babies. Only once Ellie and Sarah are born can we accurately determine exactly what we're dealing with. All of the ultrasounds and X-rays to date don't show us everything, hence we need to be as prepared as possible.'

Even now, as Janessa focused on working alongside him, Kaycee putting little knitted beanies on the babies' heads—one that had 'Ellie' stitched in and the other 'Sarah', so that staff could tell the girls apart—she recalled Miles's instructions.

'One-minute Apgar?' he asked.

'Five for Sarah. Four for Ellie,' Ray reported.

'Let's get them moved to the NICU.' Miles was firm, determined, completely in control of the situation. Janessa was as much in awe of him as before. He had knowledge, he had understanding, and as Ray and Kaycee worked with the orderlies to move the girls and the equipment they were attached to out of the delivery suite, Miles quickly crossed to Sheena's side.

'You did good. I'm so proud of you for carrying them for so long. You've given them an incredible start in life.' He brushed some hair out of Sheena's eyes and smiled at her. Janessa came up and kissed her friend on the forehead.

'Miles is right. The girls are doing very well. Rest now.'

'Good advice,' Sheena remarked, her eyes closing. 'Think I'll do just that.'

They were only a few steps behind the girls and once they were settled in the NICU in a room off to the side, enclosed by a curtain to afford privacy, the observations and checks began again.

'They're both in much better health than I had hoped,' Miles remarked after the ten-minute Apgar score on both babies was a nine. They stood there, the two of them, looking at the little girls, tubes and wires attached to them, lying on their backs, arms and legs spread, the specially made cloth nappies fastened in place.

'Yes.' She nodded, looking at the little girls who

were her goddaughters. 'And they're beautiful.' The instant she said the words tears welled in her eyes, but where before she might have walked away from Miles in the hope that he wouldn't see her exhibiting such raw emotions, now she didn't bother.

He knew the truth about her past. He knew she'd lost a baby of her own and he knew, first-hand, the pain she'd suffered. Even though time had moved on, even though the world continued to revolve around them, the pain and the memories and the burning need to be a parent still continued to pulse through both of them.

'So incredibly beautiful.' She said each word slowly, carefully and with the utmost meaning. 'I love them both so much.' She smiled through the tears that were pricking at her eyes and when Miles placed his arm around her shoulders and drew her close, she didn't even think of pulling away.

He could feel the emotions coming from her, the love radiating from her for these beautiful babies... babies that weren't her own.

It seemed right and natural that he should comfort her. It seemed right and natural to stand there with her, the two of them alone for the first time since they'd arrived back at the hospital earlier in the day. The two of them, looking at two little miracles lying joined at the hip. Ellie and Sarah. Both of them breathing rapidly in the oxygen-controlled environment, the machines around them beeping and displaying their vital signs.

'It's definitely good,' he murmured.

'I can even tell them apart,' she said with a small smile. 'Look, Ellie's face isn't as round as Sarah's.'

'Where?' Miles peered closer but still didn't remove his arm from around Janessa's shoulders. He was offering her comfort, true, but he was also a red-blooded male who was powerfully attracted to this woman. The last time he'd offered her comfort he'd been able to find the strength to pull away. This time, though, he wasn't finding it easy. Was that because he couldn't stop thinking about her? Was that because she was becoming incredibly important to him? Was it simply because he'd given in to the burning desire to kiss her? Now that he knew the flavours and sweetness of her lips against his, of how her plump pink lips seemed to have been designed to fit so perfectly against his own, he wanted to keep her as close as possible.

Although she might not want to talk about their kiss, about the sensations and emotions which had been evoked, awoken as though from a long and weary sleep, Miles couldn't ignore the way he felt for Janessa any more. Where he'd thought he'd never be able to move on from Wendy's death, here he was, desperate for some sort of signal from Janessa that she felt the same way, that she'd enjoyed the kiss, that she wanted more.

Instead, he used the excuse of leaning forward to peer more closely at the baby girls, to shift his body nearer to hers, to settle her within the circle of his arms, to have the curves of her body pressed to his, moulding as though they were meant for each other.

'Just there.' She pointed, not wanting to move away from the strength of his arm about her shoulders and angling her body towards his in order to fit more snugly against him. She knew she shouldn't. She knew she should find some sort of self-discipline to ease herself away from him, to draw back, to create distance between them because it would be far too easy to continue to snuggle in closer, especially now she knew how powerful and masterful he could be when his mouth was pressed to hers.

As though his thoughts mirrored her own, Miles angled her even closer and when she glanced up at him, it was the easiest thing in the world to lower his head a fraction, close the short distance between them and capture her lips once more in a kiss.

This time there was no initial surprise, his senses recalling with perfect clarity how she tasted. This time there were no flying goggles to distract them so they could focus on the powerful explosion of desire that existed between them. This time it was even more perfect than before.

She almost sighed into him as he once more brought her body to life. When she'd dated in the past, when she'd been interested in other men, she'd always managed to stay in complete control of her emotions. Not so with Miles. He seemed to have burst into her life, strapped her to a seat and taken her for a ride she hadn't known existed.

She'd been a pilot for many years. She'd competed in aerobatic competitions and done a multitude of extreme sports, such as parachuting, hang-gliding and para-sailing. She loved the sensation of being up in the air, of losing herself to the experience and exhilaration of such activities, but none had prepared her for the way she felt when being this close to Miles Trevellion.

Her breathing increased, her heart pummelled a wild rhythm against her chest, her mouth ardently seeking his, wanting to match him moment by moment, her knees beginning to weaken as he continued to create havoc with her equilibrium.

She was vulnerable. She was emotional. She was becoming too close to a man who would one day leave her world. She'd thought she'd been in love with Bradley all those years ago but she'd been a young and naïve teenager. She hadn't listened to the advice of those closest to her and then disaster had struck. Her son had died, her marriage had ended and then her mother had been taken from her.

Control had been her answer. To gain control over her life, she'd set off on a career of medicine, determined to specialise in the neonatal field to be able to help others. She'd worked hard, keeping any possible romantic connections strictly under control…until Miles had burst into her life.

Earlier today, this man's mouth had been wreaking havoc with her senses, just as it was now, and she was loving every moment of it. Kissing Miles, having his mouth on hers was like a dream come true, and it was a dream she'd had every night since he'd first arrived, since that first accidental kiss.

She was enjoying, far too much, the way he made her feel, the way his mouth seemed to know exactly how to tease and elicit a response. She could feel the way he appeared to be straining to keep himself under control, to keep things slow and steady, but it was there…the powerful, hot and heavy need to draw her even closer, to take the natural chemistry that existed between them out for a spin.

That was why she had to pull back. That was why she needed distance from him. He was starting to break down the heavy protective wall she'd built around herself, to keep her safe from ever giving her heart to another. The way he made her feel wasn't just physical attraction—it was an attraction of their souls. Miles understood her, appreciated her, respected her, and those special qualities would be able to completely expose her heart if she wasn't careful.

When she'd accepted the position as head of NICU years ago, Sheena had been adamant that it had been time for Janessa to start dating. Reluctantly Janessa had agreed but after about a year of the odd date here and there, her father's illness had required her attention and she'd split her time between caring for him and working round the clock at the hospital.

And now she had Ellie and Sarah. Two beautiful, precious, wonderful babies to help care for. It wasn't going to be an easy road. She knew she'd have to be there to support Sheena, to be strong for her friend, but when Miles held her like this, kissed her like this, when he touched her, held her hand, offered comfort, she wanted this to last for ever. She would be there to support Sheena and Miles could be there to support her. Couldn't he?

She knew that he would leave—eventually—and that if she did rely on him to renew her strength, she would run the risk of being even more hurt than she had been all those years ago when her marriage had failed.

Miles was kissing her. He'd opened a part of her she'd thought she'd locked securely away, and she knew, she knew full well that if she didn't start finding a way to distance herself from him, there was a fair chance she'd fall in love with him before she'd realised it.

Dangerous. The man was dangerous. Dangerous, powerful and overwhelmingly addictive.

Even though the kiss felt as though it had lasted an eternity, in reality it had been less than a minute. Janessa eased back, resting her head against his chest for a moment as she allowed her breathing to return to normal. She looked at the girls. The two darlings lying there, sleeping, their machines beeping in a steady and controlled rhythm. Thank goodness their eyes had been closed and they hadn't seen their Aunty Janessa kissing their Uncle Miles. It took another moment of gathering her strength before she pulled back, turning away from him.

'Everything all right?' Miles asked, his deep tone filled with desire.

'We need to monitor the girls.' Her tone was more brisk than she'd intended but even though the kiss hadn't lasted that long, she felt guilty at giving in to her weakness for Miles when she'd been supposed to be monitoring the girls.

'The girls are fine. In fact, they're better than fine.'

His voice was calm but his words were insistent. 'They're about the healthiest set of conjoined twins I've seen delivered in quite a few years. Janessa, we need to talk.'

She glanced at him. 'We can't, Miles,' she said softly, surprised at the huskiness of her own voice.

'Can't?'

'You know what I'm talking about.'

'Do I?'

'Please? Don't do this.'

'Do what? Question you? Comfort you? Hold you? Kiss you?' He raked a hand through his hair, knowing full well that what she was saying was the right thing to do but not wanting to do it.

'All of the above.' She spread her arms wide, shifting around to the side of the humidicrib, putting a bit more distance between them. She pretended to check the machines, to be doing anything other than standing there, looking at him. Especially when the pull to return to his arms, to press her entire body against his, to run her fingers through his hair, to urge his head down until their mouths met in hot and hungry passion were becoming the only thoughts in her mind.

'We can't.' She kept her back to him, knowing that if she looked at him, she would give in. She wasn't as strong as people thought. 'We're colleagues and we have a busy few months ahead of us with the girls and getting ready for their many surgeries.'

'Do you know how many women I've kissed since my wife died?'

'Miles.' She looked at him, even though she'd just told herself not to. 'Don't.' She shook her head, definitely not wanting to know the answer. Even the thought of him with another woman made her insides twist with distaste and jealousy, and that was precisely the reason why she needed to keep her distance from him.

'One. You. That's it. Wendy passed away seven years ago and you're the first woman I've been really interested in since.' He gestured at the distance between them. 'This sort of thing, this instant attraction, doesn't happen every day, you know.'

'I know. Do you think I don't know that? But you're in my head, Miles. You're clouding my thought processes and right now I need to keep them focused on the girls. They need me. Sheena needs me. Being around you, when you touch me, hold me, comfort me…kiss me…' She'd said the last words softly, looking away from him, unable to continue to look into those hypnotic blue eyes of his. 'You mix things up.' She took another half-step away.

'I don't know what it is that exists between us and quite frankly I don't want to know because I don't have the time for it. And neither, for that matter, do you. We've run out of time and now we have a job to do. You came to Adelaide Mercy for a very specific reason.' She pointed to the small little girls. 'Two very specific reasons, and you have the knowledge and the know-how to lead this team forward so that these little darlings can enjoy happy and normal lives. Then you and I will go our separate ways. You'll head off to the next set of conjoined twins who need your expertise and I'll stay here to help Sheena in every way I can.'

'And we'll never know what this frighteningly natural chemistry that exists between us means?'

'Exactly.'

'And what if I'm not happy about that? What if I don't agree to your terms?'

'Then that's tough.'

Miles couldn't believe what she was saying and neither could he believe how much her words were hurting him. He'd grown close to her, he'd been intrigued by her, he'd come to admire her, and yet, as she stood on the opposite side of the small private room from him, it felt as though she was skewering his heart with the sharpest scalpel in the world.

CHAPTER ELEVEN

Two weeks later, as Janessa and Kaycee finished returning the twins to their special crib after Sheena had finished cuddling them, making sure all the tubes and wires weren't twisted and everything was in the right places, Janessa came and sat by her friend. It might be two o'clock in the morning, but being here in the NICU meant she didn't have to be in her apartment, listening to Miles, thinking about Miles, dreaming about Miles.

Since the day the girls had been born, both of them had ensured that they were never left alone in a room, that they sat as far away from each other as they could during the continued meetings pertaining to Ellie's and Sarah's separation operations.

'They're so incredibly beautiful,' Sheena said, looking at her daughters with complete awe. 'I look at them and can't understand why Jonas wouldn't ever want to have children and how he could possibly disown his own daughters.' She shook her head.

'He wasn't strong enough. Not like you,' Janessa answered.

'Probably. You know, lying there in that hospital bed, being an incubator, definitely gave me a lot of time to think.'

'And?'

'And a lot of the pain and heartbreak and disbelief I felt when Jonas left isn't worth dwelling on. He was weak, selfish and stubborn. Definitely not the sort of father a mother would want for her special girls.'

'And they are special.' Janessa sighed as she looked at them. 'You're right, Sheena. It's not worth dwelling on.'

'I know I have my work cut out for me. Single mother. Raising twins. On her own.'

'You won't be alone,' Janessa protested strongly. 'You are *not* alone.'

'Oh, I know I have everyone's support here at the hospital, but people come and go, they have their own lives, their own problems. The bottom line is these are my girls. My girls. Isn't that amazing? They're my babies. No one can take them away from me. Not ever.' Sheena sighed and looked at her babies with complete adoration. 'They're mine.'

A lump sprang instantly to Janessa's throat at Sheena's words. *No one can take them away from me*. Sheena had her babies and while Sheena would share and need help and support from Janessa, the fact still remained. They were *Sheena's* babies. Not *hers*.

'Anyway…' Janessa said, pushing the pain away, determined not to intrude on Sheena's wonderful moment. Her friend deserved so much happiness, so much love, so much joy and now she had it. 'Now that the girls are fed, changed and sleeping, I'd better go do a round of the nursery and get caught up on some of my paperwork.'

'Nessa? Are you all right?' Sheena asked, yawning a little.

'I'm fine. Make sure you don't stay too long. You need your rest, too, Mummy.'

Sheena smiled at the title. 'I will, but I'd like to stay a little longer and just watch them sleep. They're such angels.'

'OK.' With that Janessa headed out into the NICU, checked on a few other babies and then headed to her office, and throughout the entire time Sheena's words were in her mind, repeating themselves over and over, niggling at her.

Ellie and Sarah were *Sheena's* babies.

Janessa didn't deny her friend the happiness of saying those words but at the same time they pierced her soul, dredging up her painful past. She hadn't been so lucky.

Pressing her hands to her temples, she could feel the beginnings of a bad headache coming on...a migraine. She hadn't had one in well over a decade. Terrible, stressful, debilitating migraines. If she didn't take care and head straight to bed, she'd be useless in the string of meetings scheduled to start at nine o'clock next morning.

Knowing it was the right thing to do, she ignored her paperwork, said goodnight to Kaycee and the other night-shift nurses, pleased to hear that Sheena had just returned to Maternity, before heading out of the NICU.

They're my babies. No one can take them away from me.

The closer she was to the residential wing, the more Sheena's words seemed to turn in her mind. It was as though hearing them had unlocked the past, unlocked the memories of her son, memories she didn't want to remember.

When she exited the stairwell on the third floor, she tried to be as quiet as she could, not wanting to wake Miles. It was as though they were sharing a house where none of the rooms actually interconnected but they could hear everything that happened.

The pounding in her head was becoming quite

fierce now and she walked carefully to the kitchenette, drawing her emergency medical kit from
the cupboard. She had nothing stronger than
paracetamol, but for now that would have to do.

*They're my babies. No one can take them away
from me.*

The words repeated as though on a constant loop,
and Janessa was unable to choke back a loud sob.
She tried to fill a glass with water in order to take
the tablets but found her hand was shaking too
much, the water sloshing everywhere. She put the
glass down before it slipped from her hand, pain
piercing her heart so intensely that she wasn't sure
she would ever breathe properly again.

Sliding to the floor, she hugged her knees and
started to cry, the pounding in her head becoming
worse with every stifled noise she made. The pressure, the pain, the pounding…on and on they went,
before she could take the throbbing around her mind
no more and, dashing to the bathroom, was violently
ill.

Rinsing her mouth and brushing her teeth, she
was startled when Miles called through the wall,
'Janessa? Are you all right?'

'I'm fine,' she called back, not wanting him to
intrude on her pain. She was trying to keep her
distance from him, trying to make sure she didn't

get hurt by not becoming involved with him on a personal level. 'Didn't mean to wake you. Go back to bed.'

Her vulnerability was at an all-time high right now, and if Miles came over, if he held her, if he—

The sound of her front door opening caused her heart to jump into her throat.

'Janessa?'

'Miles? How did you get in? The door was locked. I checked it. I made sure,' she said, walking out of the bathroom, catching a glimpse of her red eyes and blotchy skin in the mirror, to find him standing in her front hallway.

'My key works in your lock. No doubt yours works in mine but none of that is relevant right now.' He walked towards her, taking in her features. 'You were sick. Are you all right? Did you eat something wrong? Have you been injured?' He reached out for her but she backed away.

'I'm fine. Go back to bed.' It was only as she said the words that she realised he was dressed in a pair of denim jeans, a T-shirt still clasped loosely in one hand, as though he hadn't had time to dress in his rush to get to her. 'I didn't mean to disturb your sleep.'

'Janessa?' Miles was now clearly puzzled. It was obvious that she wanted him to leave but it was also obvious that she wasn't being completely truthful with him. 'It's clear that, contrary to what you're saying, you are not *fine*—in fact, you're quite pale.'

'Ugly, you mean.' She turned her back to him, not wanting to look at the incredible sight he made. She walked through to her room, now just wanting to lie down on her bed and cry herself to sleep.

'No. A little red around the eyes maybe, but most definitely not ugly.' There was a strength to his words and she wanted to believe him. Instead, she kicked off her shoes and climbed into her bed, laying her head on the pillow and closing her eyes.

'I just need sleep. You let yourself in. You can let yourself out.'

'So you're not sick?'

'If it's the meeting you're worried about, don't be. I'll be there at nine o'clock sharp.'

'I don't care about the meeting, Janessa.' There was impatience in his tone and she opened her eyes to look at him, very grateful that he'd at least put his T-shirt on and covered his tempting upper body. 'I care about *you*.'

'Well, don't.'

'Why? It's not something I can switch on and off any time I feel like it. You know there's this thing between us…this attraction that we're both working so desperately to fight.'

'I thought it was merely an attraction. I didn't know there was caring involved.' Her words were careless and tired but they triggered an immediate reaction when Miles closed the distance between them and lifted her into a sitting position, his hands firm on her arms but not to the point where he was hurting her.

'Of course I care about you. How could I not when I can't stop thinking about you? Don't you have any idea how you get to me, how you manage to get under my skin, to disturb my train of thought? I sit in meetings and all I can think about is you. I see you in the NICU and I can't help but wonder what it would be like to kiss you again. You're turning my thoughts from my work and driving me insane.' He gave her a little shake, exasperation flooding through him.

'I know we've both been doing our best to avoid each other but it's clear that there's something wrong. You were sick. I could hear you courtesy of the thin walls and terrible plumbing pipes.' His hands had gentled now and she could feel the exasperation change to the strong awareness that seemed to exist permanently between them. 'What happened? Is there something wrong in the NICU? What is it, Janessa? Are the girls OK?'

'They're fine. Better than fine. So gorgeous and

strong and healthy and…alive.' On the last word, all the strength seemed to leave her and she sagged against Miles. 'They're so alive, Miles. So alive. Not like my little boy at all. He died.'

The tears slid down her cheeks and Miles immediately gathered her to him, shifting them around so that he could sit up against the headboard of the bed and hold Janessa close.

'My Connor,' she said between hiccups. 'I couldn't face holding him. The staff were wonderful, caring and doing all they could for us. They tried to encourage me to hold him, to say goodbye, to achieve closure, but right then and there I…I couldn't. I felt so weak, so useless, so scared.'

'Oh, Nessa,' he whispered, feeling her pain.

'Then, later on, I couldn't sleep. The nurse on the ward was wonderful and when she asked me if I wanted to try and say goodbye to Connor, I agreed. She arranged everything, she was amazing. I was escorted down to the mortuary, to the small viewing room, and…I saw him. I held him. My baby. So still. So cold.' Janessa sniffed. 'So…lifeless.' She shook her head, her words barely audible. 'I was too young. My life with Bradley was over. We just couldn't get past the loss of our baby. And then…my mum died. My beautiful, sweet, loving mum. I lost so much.'

Miles listened to her talk, stroking her hair, hearing her heartbreak in every word she spoke. It was obvious she hadn't dealt with the pain of her past… but, then, until he'd met her, neither had he. He'd just forged ahead, putting his past away. He knew how she felt but at least, being there for her, holding her, helping her…hopefully she'd be able to move forward, just as she'd helped him to start letting go of his own past.

'After I buried Connor, the doctor said it wasn't wise to try for another pregnancy too soon. Bradley and I…we were both so young and in pain. We took it out on each other, blamed each other, but in the end we knew we would never be able to go back to the young carefree teenagers we'd been before Connor was born. I felt as though my life was over. That there was nothing more for me, no happily-ever-after.'

Miles shook his head. 'But you were strong. Perhaps stronger than you realised because look at what you've managed to accomplish. You went to medical school, worked hard, trained hard, no doubt determined to specialise in neonatology, to help other confused and hurting mothers. The people who have been through the same or similar experiences are the ones who can offer the most hope, the most compassion and the most understanding to those who follow. Your experiences have made you a better doctor, Nessa, even if you don't see it that way. You are a strong and incredibly intelligent woman. You're amazing.'

Janessa allowed his sweet yet strong and powerful words to wash over her, dissolving more of the protective walls she'd built around herself. Was that how he saw her? As a strong woman? Filled with compassion? Why was it that she couldn't see herself that way?

'You also looked after your father when he was ill. Sheena told me how you were his sole carer until his death.'

'And I grumbled about it at times,' she added. 'It isn't easy to look after a parent, especially when you can see their health failing right before your eyes.'

'It's not meant to be easy. The hard times only make us stronger. Easy to say, difficult to work through but still so very true.'

Janessa knew he was right and the fact that he'd been through his own heart-wrenching experiences made her listen to his words. 'So is that how you view your own negative experiences, Miles? How can you turn what happened to you into a positive?' She asked the question quietly, hiccupping a little now that her tears had stopped.

Miles rested his head against the wall and slowly exhaled. 'I don't know, Nessa, but for a while there

I had to force myself to get out of bed, to remember to breathe in and out every day, to push through the pain of my loss and try to find some sort of silver lining. My wife and son died and there was nothing I could do.'

'You were unconscious. You were hurt as well,' she pointed out, remembering what he'd told her.

'I woke up to…nothing.' He tightened his hold on her, loving the feel of her in his arms, the support and comfort she was allowing him to take from her. 'It's a day that's forever burned into my brain. The happiness of being on the train, of being with my family, of looking out the window at the incredible view, and then…nothingness.'

Janessa looked up at him, his square jaw clenched with stubbornness, his eyes staring off into the distance. 'The pain and heartbreak at being left so alone isn't a nice feeling, especially when your family was ripped from you so suddenly, but yet you went on. That takes strength.'

Miles looked down into her beautiful brown eyes, slightly red-rimmed from crying, but even so she looked gorgeous. 'What else is there to do?'

'Give up? Walk away from medicine? Change jobs? Lock yourself away? But you didn't do any of that.'

'Neither did you,' he felt compelled to point out.

Janessa gave him a crooked smile. 'A real mutual admiration society, aren't we?'

'We've got to stick together in this world.' He nodded, but his gaze dipped down to her lips.

'Yes.'

Miles swallowed and brought his free hand up to caress her cheek. 'You are so lovely, Janessa.'

She gasped at his words, her heart starting to pound wildly in her chest. She wanted him. She wanted him so badly she felt as though she was going to burst with desire. How could he elicit such emotions from her so effortlessly? Her breathing started to increase and she licked her lips as his gaze caressed her.

'I am so sorry for the pain you've been through, for what you've lost, but right now all I can think about is kissing you.'

'Oh.' The small word came out on a hiccupping breath and she found that she couldn't stop from staring into his come-hither blue eyes.

'Ever since the day the girls were born—which seems like half a lifetime ago, rather than just a few weeks—I haven't been able to stop thinking about how perfect your mouth felt against mine. About how perfectly you fit into my arms. About how perfect we are together.'

She wanted it, too. Wanted nothing more than to

follow through on her heart's desire but she paused, just for a second. 'But we can't. We work together. We have—'

Miles shook his head and placed a finger across her lips, stopping her words. 'Shh. I don't want to rationalise this, Janessa. I've spent too much time trying to figure things out, trying to deny the way being near you makes me feel, but the truth of the matter is that you make me feel alive again.

'For the past seven years since Wendy's death, I've been existing, going from one job to the next, in order to help out where I could but also to close myself off from the world. It's easy to move through the world, to appear fine and healthy when you know how. You smile, you nod, you provide your expertise. You receive thanks, you shake hands, you go on your way, heading off to the next place where you do it all again. No one gets close enough to touch the real you, deep down inside. Everyone is kept at arm's length. Everything is under control. Or at least that's how my life was…until I met you.' His finger outlined her trembling lips and Janessa's eyelids fluttered closed as she accepted the caress.

'Miles.' His name was a breathless whisper. 'I want this, too, but—'

'You don't want to get hurt when I leave,' he finished for her, shifting slightly to bring her a little closer to him.

'Yes.' She opened her eyes and looked directly into his.

'I can't promise anything, Janessa, only that I want to spend more time with you, to hold you close, to kiss you. I never thought I would *ever* become interested in a woman again and the fact that I have, the fact that I want you, that I can't stop thinking about you, that I want to kiss you every time I see you, is a miracle within itself. I didn't think I had the capacity to care for anyone as deeply as I do for you.'

'So…what are you saying? That you'll stay? That you'll remain in Adelaide once the girls have been separated? That you want to keep seeing me? Spending time with me?'

Miles looked down at her mouth, tempted to lie, to promise her whatever she wanted, just so he could kiss those perfect lips of hers…but he knew he couldn't. She'd been hurt so long ago and the fact that she was still so incredibly cautious only showed him just how deep that hurt had gone. It also showed him that he owed her one thing right now, and that was the complete truth.

'It's tempting, Nessa. So very tempting, and that in itself is something new. I've always been in control, had things mapped out, known exactly what's happening next, but not now.' He spoke so clearly, so articulately, and it was just another facet to him that she was coming to love.

Love?

Janessa ignored the thought, focusing on the here and now because on a romantic level the 'here and now' always ended with a generous serving of pain and sadness later on. Why was it that he had to go? Why did he have to leave? To move? Wasn't it worthwhile, staying here? Seeing whether these wonderful sensations that had existed between them since they'd first met meant anything?

'Janessa?' Miles saw confusion, anxiousness and longing cross her face, and he knew she was just as confused as he was. 'You once asked me if there was any hope for a "happily ever after" for control freaks such as us.'

'Mm-hm?'

'I think there might be.'

'Really?' She edged closer, hope filling her heart as she leaned up towards his mouth, wanting more than the touch of his fingers on her neck, her cheeks, her lips.

'Yes.' The word was a whisper of promise. What was coursing between them, filling the room with energy and repressed tension, was too strong for either of them to cope with right now. 'I want you, Janessa. Don't ever think that I don't.'

'Show me, Miles.'

'Oh, honey, I want to.' He closed his eyes as though in pain. 'Believe me, I want to.' He brushed his thumb over her lips once more before gently easing himself away. Where he found the strength, he had no idea but now, when she'd been upset, when she was tired, when both of them had no real answers to their present dilemma, he also knew he couldn't take advantage of her. She was too special, too precious. She wasn't just *some woman*. She was an *important* woman in his life. That was the realisation he'd reached tonight and as such she deserved far more than he could presently give.

'But we both need to get some sleep.' He stood with his back to her as he collected himself, slowly exhaling before walking around the bed. 'Rest.' He reached out and brushed some hair from her forehead. 'More meetings in the morning.'

'Yes.' Janessa captured his hand in hers and sat up, kissing his knuckles. 'Thank you, Miles.'

'For?'

'For being a gentleman. For listening. For comforting.'

Miles's heart was throbbing in his chest and he clenched his jaw for another long moment, wanting her so badly but knowing it wasn't right…not yet. He gave her a crooked smile and pushed his free hand through his hair. 'Glad I could help.' He stood there for a moment, just looking at her, feeling his superhuman strength start to drain. 'Good heavens, you're beautiful,' he ground out, and then, before he succumbed, he let go of her hand and headed towards the front door.

'Miles?' Janessa was on her feet and heading after him as quickly as she could. He stopped by her open front door and spun around eagerly to face her. 'What does this mean? About us? *Is* there an us?'

He could hear, could see all her vulnerabilities. She was being open with him, allowing him to see the real Janessa, and she couldn't have given him a stronger reason to give her the answer she deserved. 'Yes. Yes, honey. Whether we like it or not, there is an *us*.' He wasn't sure how she'd take that news. They'd both verbalised their feelings, their uncertainty, their hesitation in moving forward.

Janessa nodded slowly, then took him completely by surprise when she stepped forward and wrapped her arms about him. Her body, soft and glorious against his own. 'If there really is an "us", then there's also a "we", and I think *we* should at least kiss goodnight,' she murmured, and when his arms slid eagerly around her waist, she brought his head down so their lips could meet, both of them giving in to the powerful sensations that zinged between them.

She was perfect. So sweet, so supple, so sensual. She was sugar and spice and all things nice, and yet he wasn't sure whether standing here, holding her, kissing her was the right thing to do when his need for her continued to increase.

Groaning with regret, Miles eased back after a few minutes and set her at arm's length—her inside her door, he in the corridor outside.

'Now. Get some sleep. We'll…talk more later on today.'

Janessa sighed and smiled at him, her eyelids half-closed with relaxed sensuality. 'OK.' Still, she didn't move. She just stood leaning against the wall, looking at him with a little half-smile on her lips. It was very disconcerting and extremely distracting, especially when he was trying to do the right thing.

'Uh…how about we have breakfast together?'

She nodded. 'Sounds great.'

'I have fresh fruit and bagels.'

Her smile increased. 'I'll make fresh coffee. Your place or mine?' She giggled a little and it was all Miles could do not to gather her up and close her door with him firmly on the other side of it with her. He shoved his hands into his pockets and balled them into fists.

'Yours.'

'Set your alarm clock for the usual time. I've been relying on it to wake me up for the past few weeks. Tomorrow morning shouldn't be any different.' Her smile was now wide, sleepy and inviting. He clenched his jaw so tight, his head began to ache.

'Until then.' And before he could be affected by her any more, he reached forward and pulled her door closed, effectively shutting her in and himself out. Quickly, he opened his own door and went into his apartment, being mindful to be as quiet as possible as he walked straight to the bedroom and fell onto the bed, burying his face in the pillows.

Janessa was incredible, gorgeous and driving him to distraction. The last time he'd felt this way about a woman, the last time he'd allowed a woman to get this deep beneath his carefully groomed exterior, he'd married her. He and Wendy had enjoyed a few wonderful years together but then she'd been taken from him, leaving him all alone.

Now, out of the blue, he'd found Janessa. Funny, clever, evocative Janessa, and he knew he was in real danger of losing his heart.

CHAPTER TWELVE

THEY met for breakfast the next morning, enjoying coffee, bagels and fruit whilst deciding to spend as much time together as their schedules would allow.

Ever since the safe delivery of Ellie and Sarah into the world, the planning for their first operation of inserting the tissue expanders had accelerated. The different specialists Miles had requested to assist him with the surgery would be arriving in the next few weeks. However, the major surgical procedure, the actual separation, wouldn't take place until Miles deemed the girls healthy enough to endure an intense anaesthetic.

Until then, there were still several planning sessions and extra scans to be completed. The planning for a surgical procedure for separating conjoined twins was extensive. Of course, this extra workload also meant that any free time Janessa and Miles might previously have enjoyed was sucked away by meetings and paperwork.

They also had to juggle the press, to ensure that

no one from the media could sneak into the NICU to take photographs of the twins. Charisma, the hospital CEO, was controlling this as best she could, but it meant that Sheena and the girls were often hidden away in a corner of the NICU where even the other young mothers weren't able to pry.

Official photographs had been taken of mother and daughters and Sheena had given a few interviews earlier on, and once that was out of the way they were able to focus completely on maintaining the health of the twins.

Throughout it all, Janessa and Miles tried to eat at least one meal together every day, and as they didn't keep conventional hours, sometimes they found themselves sitting in the hospital cafeteria at three o'clock in the morning, quite content to talk and share with each other.

The fact that Miles knew of her past, knew of her heartbreak and the inner turmoil she'd experienced only made it easier for her to talk to him. He understood. He'd been in a similar position and by the same token she found herself wanting to know about his life, wanting to know where he went to medical school, how often he saw his parents and siblings.

Sometimes he looked as though he was about to clam up, to not give a straight answer to what she wanted to know, but every time he would take a breath and talk. He was so generous and it also showed Janessa that he really was invested in the 'us' that existed between them.

Still, they continued to take things one step at a time. They enjoyed spending time with each other and they enjoyed working together. The more they talked, the more they understood that this attraction, which seemed to have existed between them almost from the instant they'd met, was only intensifying with each passing moment.

Still, she knew their time together was limited. Miles was a man of great skill and importance in the world of conjoined twins. His expertise would always be in demand and she had no idea where or how she would fit into any plans he might make. It was the only thing that worried her but she tried her best not to show it, putting on a brave face, being happy whenever they were together yet always waiting for that axe to fall.

'This is my favourite and worst part of the day,' Miles said one evening as he stood at Janessa's apartment door, drawing her into his arms.

'Well, that's not at all ambiguous,' she drawled.

'It's my favourite because I get to kiss you, but the worst because we must part.'

'You're so poetic,' she remarked as she brushed her fingers lovingly through his hair, pulling out a piece of confetti. 'Can you believe the girls are already one month old?'

'The time does seem to be flying by at the rate of knots.'

'It was so sweet of you to organise that little party for Sheena in my office.'

'Sweet?' He quirked an eyebrow at the adjective. 'Thoughtful?'

He raised the other brow.

'Masterful?' she tried, but only caused his expression to turn more quizzical. 'Stroke of genius?'

'Ah, that's better. Genius. I like the sound of that one.'

Janessa laughed, unable to believe she could be this happy as he brought her closer and captured her lips with his. She gasped a little, just as she did every time when that first electrifying contact was made. Then she would sigh and lean into him, loving the slow and perfect movement of his mouth on hers.

Miles listened to her, supported her, argued with her—when it was warranted—and held her so securely in his arms whenever he said goodnight. They were a couple and they didn't hide it. Everyone knew, and was very pleased, about this latest development between the two neonatologists.

'It's about time,' Sheena had said, happy for both her friends. 'I could tell the instant I saw the two of

you together that you were meant for each other.'
She'd clapped her hands. 'So? What happens next?
Will you be staying in Adelaide, Miles?'

'Um…' Miles had looked at Janessa, at the woman
who had the ability to fill him with the strongest
sense of belonging. 'Charisma has approached
me about extending my contract here at Adelaide
Mercy.'

'Wow.' Sheena had been surprised. 'Charisma will
no doubt do everything she can to secure your services.'

Miles had smiled and it had been then
Janessa had noted that the smile hadn't reached his
eyes. Was he possibly considering staying here at
Adelaide Mercy? To be with her? She couldn't help
but think that he'd miss the travel, miss the excitement of helping other sets of conjoined twins. He had
so much expertise and knowledge it almost seemed
a waste of talent to hold him to just one place.

Even now, as he held her in his arms, as he kissed
her so completely, so passionately, she couldn't help
but wonder if he would stay because it was what
he wanted to do, or if he was considering staying
because this was where she was?

'Well, my genius,' she murmured as she closed
her eyes and rested her head on his chest, not both-
ering to hide the fact that his kisses had made her

breathless. 'I was looking in my diary and noticed that on Friday afternoon both of us have a block of two whole hours where there are no meetings, no scans, no ward rounds, no anything.'

Miles frowned but there was a twinkle in his eyes as he eased her back a little to look into her glorious face. 'Really? Can that be possible? You don't actually mean we might have some…leisure time?'

Janessa laughed. 'It does look that way.'

'Hmm.' He smiled. 'What did you have in mind and does it involve your car?'

'Well, well, well. A genius and a mind-reader.'

'Airfield?'

'Airfield,' she agreed. 'You can drive the car and I'll fly the plane.'

'Sounds like a plan.'

'A plan for five days in advance.' Janessa grimaced. 'Here's hoping that nothing—'

Miles pressed a kiss to her lips, effectively cutting off her words. 'Don't even say it. Let's just hold on to the dream of Friday.' He kissed her again, then put her from him. 'Sleep sweet, my Nessa.'

'See you in the morning,' she replied as she reluctantly eased from his arms. Leaning against the door after she'd closed it, she hugged her arms close, feeling bereft of his touch. She loved him so much and she wondered if she had the strength to give him up.

A fax had been sent through to the NICU for Dr Trevellion and it had arrived on her desk along with all the other faxes for the NICU. The letter had been from a hospital in the UK, requesting his valued expertise with the case of another set of conjoined twins that were due to be born around Christmas.

When she'd read the letter—purely by accident at first—her throat had gone dry and her stomach had churned, making her feel instantly ill at the thought of Miles leaving. He hadn't said a word to her about the offer and she wondered whether he was going to accept.

How could he not? He was a man with such an incredible skill and thanks to him and a team of highly skilled professionals, he was able to provide a healthy and separate existence for babies who were born conjoined. How could she possibly ask him to stay? To turn down the job in order to be with her?

How was she going to face not seeing him? Not holding him? Not being with him? Not kissing him? He was her joy, her elation, her happiness. It had taken her so long to find him and now…now that she had…she was supposed to let him go? It wasn't fair!

Hearing him shuffling around next door, she put

her hand up to the wall, knowing she would do her best to be happy, to enjoy the time they had left together. She desperately wanted—no, *needed*—to be close to him. Her Miles. Her life. Her love.

Miles pressed his hand to the wall, desperately wanting to be with Janessa. So many times during the past few weeks he'd wanted to pick up a sledgehammer and smash a hole in the wall that separated them. He wanted to be with Janessa, not just for now but for ever.

The knowledge had stunned him and it was then he'd finally admitted that his feelings for Janessa were those of love. He loved her. He'd fallen in love again and that in itself was a miracle. For far too many years his life had been lonely and empty and he'd worked hard to fill it and be satisfied within his professional life at least. Everyone in the neonate world knew of Miles Trevellion but Janessa was the only one who *knew* him.

The discussions they'd had, not only about the twins but about the advances in medical technology, the memories they'd shared of their past, of their babies whose lives had been cut so short and the painful hurt that had followed, bonded them closer. He recalled the quiet, reflective moments when they'd been flying in her Tiger Moth, looking at the calm scenery below, relaxing in each other's company.

All of these moments, such as holding her close, offering comfort when they'd been unable to save little Philip or after their first meal together when she'd turned her head and his lips had been pressed to hers in a glorious tantalising accident...they were all perfect and wonderful and he wanted so desperately to stay, to be with Janessa, to make more memories, to move forward with his life rather than going around in circles.

Earlier that day, he'd received a phone call from the hospital in the UK, the same hospital that had faxed over an invitation for him to lead a team of neonatologists in separating the next case of conjoined twins, which had only just been diagnosed. The hospital director had been insistent for Miles to accept as soon as possible. The sooner planning could start, the better—but for the first time in seven years he'd hesitated, and he'd hesitated because of Janessa.

For the first time he had been unsure of what to do, of what was best—not for his patients—but for *him*. Spending time with Janessa, holding her, being with her, kissing her... If he left, if he accepted the job offer, he wouldn't be able to do any of those things.

She'd once asked him what he was running away from, why he travelled so much. At the time he'd been unwilling to give her an in-depth answer but now that he'd had some time to really think about it, he realised he hadn't been running away from anything but rather running towards her. He hadn't known it at the time, of course. Travelling and being busy had most certainly helped his mental thought processes to deal with the loss of his wife and child, but after seven years he was ready to start living again and he wanted to do that living with Janessa.

On Friday, Janessa tiptoed her way gingerly through the morning, almost waiting for something to go wrong, for the block of time she and Miles had set aside to be eaten up with something else—but it wasn't.

'Go and enjoy,' Sheena said as she finished expressing some breast milk. Both of the girls were starting to put on weight and soon the first of their many surgeries would begin. 'We're all doing just fine here. It's time you and Miles spent some time away from the hospital.'

'Yes.' Janessa frowned.

'Something wrong?' Sheena asked as she buttoned up her shirt.

'Nothing. Everything.'

'Oh. Is that all? Come on. This is me, Nessa. Don't you think that I can't see straight through you?'

'I love him, Sheenie.' The words came out on a sigh, a sad sigh, filled with resignation.

'You don't sound too happy about it.'

'We can never be together.' She spoke as though there was no hope for tomorrow. To even contemplate a life without Miles made her heart constrict with pain, it made her stomach twist into knots and it made her want to sit all day and do nothing. Without Miles, she felt her life would lose all meaning.

'What?' Sheena sat up straight and glared at her friend. 'Why ever not?'

'He's been offered another job.'

'Great. He's a man of talent and skill. It's not an uncommon occurrence. What's the problem?'

'What's the problem?' Janessa sprang to her feet, needing to pace, but there was no room—the small NICU cubicle had no room. 'The problem is that I want him to stay here in Adelaide, with *me*. I can't let him do that.'

'Why not?'

'Because there are other little babies out there who need his expertise. He's so brilliant and incredible at what he does that I can't let him stop doing it just because I want him to be with me. That's a little selfish, don't you think?'

'So…go with him.'

Janessa paused. 'What?'

'Go with him.'

'But…uh…what about you? The girls? My friends? My job? My house has almost finished being built. What about that?'

'Oh, nonsense. All of that is irrelevant. Now that you've met Miles and fallen in love with him, *he* should be your first priority. Not me.'

'But, Sheena, I promised I would always be here to help you.'

'And you will. It doesn't mean that you can't do something else for a while. Why not go with Miles? Help out as part of his team of experts. You're more than qualified and now, because of Ellie and Sarah, you'll have had experience in this elite field.' Sheena laughed. 'Nessa, the girls are going to be spending the rest of this year, at least, in this hospital. They're going to be well cared for and we both know I'll be fine. First I was their incubator. Now I'm their snack machine.' Sheena rolled her eyes and laughed at herself before standing and crossing to Janessa's side.

'If you love Miles—*really* love him, Ness—then you do what you need to do to be happy. Don't you go thinking about me or the girls or the hospital or your house. None of us are going anywhere and we'll always be here for you, just as we know you'll always be there for us.'

Janessa listened to what her friend was saying and sighed. 'OK. Let's say, for a start that Miles does want me to go with him to the UK, to be a part of his team. What happens when *that* case is finished and he gets offered *another* case? You forget. I've been following this man's career for years. I've read the articles he writes for the leading neonate journals, I know he likes to move around. It's who he is. It's what he does.'

'It's what he *did*.' Sheena's smile broadened. 'I've seen the way you look at him and I've seen the way he looks at you, and I have to say that both of my friends have been bitten by the same bug. The love bug.' She wiggled her fingers at Janessa as she said the words but Janessa just couldn't smile at the action, her insides churning with confusion and indecision. Sheena instantly sobered and gave her friend a hug.

'This isn't a bad thing, Ness. It's a good thing. You've fallen in love. For real this time. You're not an impulsive teenager any more. This is real and good and right and everything else that's wonderful.'

Janessa stood there and processed Sheena's words, realising that true happiness might well be within her grasp. That if what Sheena said was true, if

Miles cared for her as much as she cared for him, there might be the slightest hope that they could work things out.

'I have to go find him.'

'Atta-girl,' Sheena said with a wide grin on her face. She watched her friend blow a kiss to the sleeping twins and race out of the NICU.

Janessa had arranged to meet Miles at her car, and after quickly changing she headed to the old shed behind the residential wing. He'd already opened the double doors in order to drive the car out and for a moment she couldn't see him.

She paused, her gaze searching frantically for him. Was he here? He had to be here. They were supposed to meet here. And then she caught sight of him, bent down low next to the car, rag in hand, giving the paintwork a polish. Her heart turned over with love for him.

She stood there, watching the way his muscles flexed beneath his shirt, the way his legs were powerful and strong, the way he cared for her car in exactly the same way as her father had. He was a kind, caring and considerate man and she was instantly struck with overwhelming regret that her father had never been able to meet this most extraordinary man.

'Hey,' he said when he looked up and saw her. 'Just giving her the once-over. Almost ready to go.' When Janessa didn't move, Miles stopped what he was doing and tossed the rag back onto the work bench. 'Is everything all right? The twins? Sheena?'

'They're fine. Everything's fine. We're good to go. But…do you mind if we take a slight detour first? It's not far. About two blocks from here.'

'OK. Sure.' He opened the passenger door for her, pressing a quick kiss to her lips before hurrying around to slide behind the wheel. They both put on their seat belts and Miles turned the key in the ignition, the engine purring instantly to life. 'Oh, yeah. This car is the best.'

Janessa just smiled as she gave him directions. Soon they pulled up outside a house that was almost finished being built. There were a few workmen around, banging and hammering, but apart from the unfinished landscaping, the house looked almost complete. They climbed from the car and then leaned against it.

'This is my house,' she said to Miles. 'My new house,' she clarified. 'The other one burnt down.'

He nodded. 'I remember Sheena saying something about that on the day we met.'

Janessa sighed, allowing him to pull her into his

arms, snuggling in as close as possible. 'It seems so long ago. That first day.'

'A lot has happened,' he agreed, thinking of the way he loved her so completely.

'Yes.' They stood there for a few minutes, just watching, both of them lost in their thoughts. Finally, it was Miles who broke the silence.

'Is this where you think we should live?'

'Well…' She looked up at him and eased away. 'Yes and no.'

'Great. Not ambiguous at all.' He took her hands in his and studied her closely. She linked her fingers with his and squeezed their hands, wanting to bind them together for ever.

'Miles…these past few weeks that we've been together have been the happiest of my life for many, *many* years. Even before that, from the moment you walked into my NICU, being bossy and demanding and jet-lagged…telling me I looked too young to run a NICU—'

'Young and beautiful and way too tempting for a man who was completely exhausted,' he interjected.

'Well, yes.' She smiled at his words, feeling her cheeks get a little hot. He chuckled at her embarrassment and brushed a kiss across her lips. 'Miles, what I'm trying to say, very badly, is that…' She paused and took a deep breath. 'I don't think you should stay.'

'What? At the residential wing any more? Do you think we should move in here, to the house?'

'No. That's not what I meant.' She took another deep breath. 'What I mean is...I know about the job,' she confessed. 'The fax you received was mixed up with my faxes, and I'm afraid I was halfway through reading it before I realised it wasn't for me. I'm sorry. I should have said something earlier.'

'The job in the UK?'

'Yes.'

'I wasn't going to mention it.'

'Why not?'

'Because I'm not going.'

'But you *have* to. Those babies *need* you.'

'You want me to go? To leave Adelaide?' He swallowed over the sudden dryness in his throat. Didn't she want him? He was positive that she loved him, even though she hadn't said the words...yet. Was that why she'd brought him to her house? To show him that she would be fine, living here, without him?

'Miles, you are so incredibly talented and there are babies in the world who need you.'

'More than you?' The words were asked quietly, softly but earnestly.

Janessa slowly shook her head, her eyes intent.

'No, but I can't be selfish. I can't keep you all for myself. It's your own fault for being so terrific.'

'I see.' He thought for a moment. 'So you're saying I should take the job in the UK? That I should go and help those little babies?'

'Yes.'

'Because you can't be selfish?'

'No.'

'Because you love me?'

'Yes.' She gasped, only realising belatedly what she'd said. She met his gaze and found his eyes twinkling with delight.

'Well…if that's the case, then I'll definitely have to accept that job and I'll also let the hospital know that I'll be bringing you along with me.'

'Really? You want me to go with you?'

He stared at her, an incredulous look on his face. 'Why would you think I'd go *anywhere* without you?' he asked, and it was only then that she heard the tenderness in his tone. 'I need you, Janessa.'

'What?'

'I need you,' he repeated, and tugged her back into his arms. 'It doesn't matter whether I'm working at Adelaide Mercy or in the UK or in Timbuktu! If I'm with you, I'll be happy. I had planned to talk to you about all of this at the airfield. I even thought of having someone sky-write a note asking you to marry me. But when I called Myrna and enquired about sky-writing, she said you were the pilot who usually did that.'

'Ma-ma-marry?' Janessa was stuck on the one word.

'Janessa, honey. I love you.' His words were plain, simple, straightforward. Good, old-fashioned honesty. That was what she was getting, and a slow smile crept onto her lips.

'You love me?'

'Are you going to keep asking questions or are you going to answer some?'

'Uh…sorry.' She gave her head a little shake, needing to clear it in order to take in everything he was saying. Miles loved her! He wanted to marry her! 'Of course I'll answer questions. What questions would you like me to answer?'

'Do you really love me?'

'Oh, Miles. Yes. Yes, I do. I have for quite some time now, although I couldn't admit it to myself. I was too scared to say anything in case you didn't feel the sa—'

Miles silenced her the best, most enjoyable way he knew how. Janessa instantly gave herself up to his kisses, leaning into him and wrapping her arms tightly about him. 'Nessa,' he groaned when they finally broke apart. 'You will marry me, won't you?'

'Yes. How could you doubt that?'

He kissed her again and once more received no complaints. 'And you will come to the UK with me?'

'I'd follow you to the ends of the earth. I don't mind if we travel because home is where the heart is…and my heart belongs to you.' She kissed him.

'And I don't mind,' he said, 'if we stay put for a while. It's been a very long time since I've put down roots and, thanks to you, I'm ready to start again.' He indicated the house in front of them. 'A new home for a new beginning.'

'Yes. Although I don't think Charisma will be too happy at the cha—'

Miles kissed her, cutting her words off once more.

'Are you just trying to cut me off so you can—?'

Another kiss.

'Miles!'

Another kiss before he laughed. 'I'll take any excuse I can to kiss my fiancée,' he remarked.

'Fiancée?' Janessa blinked slowly at the realisation.

'You *did* just agree to marry me, didn't you?'

'Yes. Yes, I did.'

'Excellent news.' He paused. 'You do realise I'm not just asking you to join me overseas because I love you.'

She raised her eyebrows. 'There are more reasons?'

'Yes. You're a highly skilled neonatologist and I'd be insane to pass up this opportunity to ask you to join the team. I know,' he continued quickly, 'that it will mean applying for leave from Adelaide Mercy and leaving the family you've gathered around you, but we'll return. We'll be back. After we've finished in the UK, we can return to Adelaide.'

'What if another case of conjoined twins comes up? Miles, I don't want to hold you back. You're incredible with the way you work, the way you care, your expertise.'

'We can assess things on a case by case basis together...at least until we're ready to have children of our own.' The words were said quietly...more quietly than anything else he'd said.

'You want children?'

'Don't you?'

'Yes. Yes, I do. I want to have children with you, Miles.' Her tone was quiet but he could hear the veiled fear behind her words.

'We'll make sure everything goes smoothly. We have the best resources, the best teams right here at Adelaide Mercy,' he encouraged. 'The point is that whatever we face, we'll face it together.'

She nodded in agreement, feeling his strength and certainty flow through her. No longer would they be alone. Together they would make a new family, a second chance at love and life. With Miles by her side, Janessa knew there wasn't anything she couldn't face, and she smiled up at the man of her dreams—her fiancé.

'Together,' she agreed, and knew that all her dreams really would come true.

* * * * *

Mills & Boon® Large Print Medical

March

CORT MASON – DR DELECTABLE — Carol Marinelli
SURVIVAL GUIDE TO DATING YOUR BOSS — Fiona McArthur
RETURN OF THE MAVERICK — Sue MacKay
IT STARTED WITH A PREGNANCY — Scarlet Wilson
ITALIAN DOCTOR, NO STRINGS ATTACHED — Kate Hardy
MIRACLE TIMES TWO — Josie Metcalfe

April

BREAKING HER NO-DATES RULE — Emily Forbes
WAKING UP WITH DR OFF-LIMITS — Amy Andrews
TEMPTED BY DR DAISY — Caroline Anderson
THE FIANCÉE HE CAN'T FORGET — Caroline Anderson
A COTSWOLD CHRISTMAS BRIDE — Joanna Neil
ALL SHE WANTS FOR CHRISTMAS — Annie Claydon

May

THE CHILD WHO RESCUED CHRISTMAS — Jessica Matthews
FIREFIGHTER WITH A FROZEN HEART — Dianne Drake
MISTLETOE, MIDWIFE...MIRACLE BABY — Anne Fraser
HOW TO SAVE A MARRIAGE IN A MILLION — Leonie Knight
SWALLOWBROOK'S WINTER BRIDE — Abigail Gordon
DYNAMITE DOC OR CHRISTMAS DAD? — Marion Lennox

Mills & Boon® Large Print Medical

June

NEW DOC IN TOWN	Meredith Webber
ORPHAN UNDER THE CHRISTMAS TREE	Meredith Webber
THE NIGHT BEFORE CHRISTMAS	Alison Roberts
ONCE A GOOD GIRL…	Wendy S. Marcus
SURGEON IN A WEDDING DRESS	Sue MacKay
THE BOY WHO MADE THEM LOVE AGAIN	Scarlet Wilson

July

THE BOSS SHE CAN'T RESIST	Lucy Clark
HEART SURGEON, HERO…HUSBAND?	Susan Carlisle
DR LANGLEY: PROTECTOR OR PLAYBOY?	Joanna Neil
DAREDEVIL AND DR KATE	Leah Martyn
SPRING PROPOSAL IN SWALLOWBROOK	Abigail Gordon
DOCTOR'S GUIDE TO DATING IN THE JUNGLE	Tina Beckett

August

SYDNEY HARBOUR HOSPITAL: LILY'S SCANDAL	Marion Lennox
SYDNEY HARBOUR HOSPITAL: ZOE'S BABY	Alison Roberts
GINA'S LITTLE SECRET	Jennifer Taylor
TAMING THE LONE DOC'S HEART	Lucy Clark
THE RUNAWAY NURSE	Dianne Drake
THE BABY WHO SAVED DR CYNICAL	Connie Cox